THE PLEASURES OF LOVE

Only little boys and old men sneer at love.
      Louis Auchincloss

By the same editor

The Marriage Quotation Book
The Pleasures of the Table
The Gourmet Quotation Book
The Wine Quotation Book
The Gardener's Quotation Book
The Traveller's Quotation Book

The Pleasures of Love

Edited by
JENNIFER TAYLOR

ROBERT HALE · LONDON

Preface and selection © Jennifer Taylor 1994
First published in Great Britain 1994

ISBN 0 7090 5243 X

Robert Hale Limited
Clerkenwell House
Clerkenwell Green
London EC1R 0HT

The right of Jennifer Taylor to be identified as
author of this work has been asserted by her
in accordance with the Copyright, Designs and
Patents Act 1988.

2 4 6 8 10 9 7 5 3 1

For S. with love

Photoset in North Wales by
Derek Doyle & Associates, Mold, Clwyd.
Printed and bound in Great Britain by
WBC Ltd, Bridgend, Mid-Glamorgan.

Contents

Preface	7
Love Is …	11
Of Men and Women	22
Of True Love	29
First Love	32
Declarations	43
Kisses	56
Happy Days	60
Obstacles	62
Separation	66
Jealousy and Obsession	73
Imbroglios	79
Rapture	82
Heartbreak	92
Of Marriage	99
Proposals	106
Rejection	118
We Are Engaged	121
Wedding Bells	128

The Honeymoon	136
Halcyon Days	143
Intimations	148
Rows	160
Affairs	165
Partings	171
Mature Love	174
Memories	180
Regrets	183
Wisdom	185
Envoi	188
Index	189

Acknowledgement

Maurice Lindsay's poem 'Love's Anniversaries', from *Collected Poems 1940–1990* (Mercat Press, Edinburgh) appears by permission of the author.

Preface

THE old saying, that love makes the world go round, is not strictly accurate; it only feels like it at times. As Franklin Jones said, it makes the ride worthwhile. Few would argue with that.

Times and manners change, but human nature and the human condition do not, and despite changed social conventions the voices and emotions of lovers centuries ago, recorded in letters or diaries, ring true with undimmed poignancy. There is a rich crop of love letters to choose from, and the only difficulty is that the sentiments expressed are inevitably a little repetitive. Lovers are voluble indeed. One of the longest lasting relationships that features in this book is that between Victor Hugo and his mistress Juliette Drouet; throughout their more than fifty years together she wrote him something like twenty thousand letters – which works out at no more than a letter a day.

Do love letters get written much, or at all, these days, when lovers apart can bill and coo down the phone to their heart's content, if not their telephone bill's? The fax is of course always available ...

Such is the speed with which relationships

progress, compared with the long courtships of old, that one might think romance has gone out of fashion. But judging from the stories related on Classic FM's Classic Romance programme every week, from the success of Robert James Waller's *The Bridges of Madison County* – a sort of updated *Brief Encounter* – and from the columns of Valentine messages in *The Times* every year, romance is alive and well with Huggybear, Ratso, Bobbles Bombom and Stinky Pooh *et al*.

Then there is almost the whole of literature which explores love in its different aspects, from the precisely charted relationships in Jane Austen to the varied range of Dickens, and from the reckless passions of Stendhal's novels to the thwarted feelings in Edith Wharton. The problem again is one of selection.

It is of course the 'true stories' which are most touching – the shy ardour of Francis Kilvert's love for the pretty Daisy, Queen Victoria's transports of delight on her honeymoon with Albert, George Sand's transports of grief at the breakup of her relationship with Alfred de Musset. And one's curiosity is stirred: how long did the relationship last? Did they live happily ever after? The answer is sometimes 'Not that long' and 'Not really', but there are nevertheless sufficient cases of long-lasting, devoted, mature love to make this a celebration of love and its pleasures.

JENNIFER TAYLOR

If love be good, from whence cometh my woe?
Geoffrey Chaucer

Love Is ...

Love is the religion of earthly happiness.
>   ALFRED DE MUSSET
>   *La Confession d'un enfant du siècle*

Love is the wine of existence.
>   HENRY WARD BEECHER
>   *Proverbs from Plymouth Pulpit*

Love is a tickling sensation around the heart.
>   AMERICAN PROVERB

Love is the poetry of the senses.
>   HONORÉ DE BALZAC
>   *Physiologie du mariage*

God is love, I dare say. But what a mischievous devil love is.
>   SAMUEL BUTLER
>   *Notebooks*

Love is a kind of warfare.
>   OVID
>   *Ars Amatoria*

Love is the strange bewilderment which overtakes one person on account of another person.
> JAMES THURBER and E.B. WHITE
> *Is Sex Necessary?*

Love, n. A temporary insanity curable by marriage or by removal of the patient from the influences under which he incurred the disorder.
> AMBROSE BIERCE
> *The Enlarged Devil's Dictionary*

Yet what is love, I pray thee sain?
It is a sunshine mixed with rain.
It is a toothache, or like pain;
It is a game where none doth gain …
> SIR WALTER RALEIGH
> 'What Is Love?'

Love conquers all things except poverty and toothache.
> MAE WEST

Love is a universal migraine
A bright stain on the vision
Blotting out reason.
> ROBERT GRAVES
> 'Symptoms of Love'

Love is a disease which begins with a fever and ends with a pain.
> AMERICAN PROVERB

Love is sentimental measles.
> CHARLES KINGSLEY

Love is a very papithatick thing as well as troubelsom and tiresome.
   MARJORY FLEMING

'Oh Edwin, kiss me, love! I'm going to be sick.'
From *Punch* in 1874.

Love is the salt of life
   AMERICAN PROVERB

Love is life, love is the lamp that lights the universe: without that light this goodly frame, the earth, is a barren promontory and man the quintessence of dust.
> MARY ELIZABETH BRADDON
> *Miranda*, 1913

You are as prone to love as the sun is to shine; it being the most delightful and natural employment of the Soul of Man: without which you are dark and miserable. For certainly he that delights not in Love makes vain the universe, and is of necessity to himself the greatest burden.
> THOMAS TRAHERNE
> *Centuries of Meditations*

There is only one happiness in life, to love and be loved.
> GEORGE SAND
> in a letter to Lina Calamatta, 31 March 1863

Love is all – love and life in the sun,
Love is the main thing, the mistress does not
  matter:
What matters the bottle so long as we get drunk?
> ALFRED DE MUSSET

Love doesn't make the world go round. Love is what makes the ride worthwhile.
> FRANKLIN P. JONES

Oh, life is a glorious cycle of song,
A medley of extemporanea;
And love is a thing that can never go wrong;
And I am Marie of Rumania.
> DOROTHY PARKER
> *Enough Rope*

I believe it doesn't exist, save as a word: a sort of wailing phoenix that is really the wind in the trees.
>D.H. LAWRENCE
>in a letter

Love is not the dying moan of a distant violin – it is the triumphant twang of a bedspring.
>attributed to S.J. PERELMAN

Love – the dirty trick nature played on us to achieve the continuation of the species.
>W. SOMERSET MAUGHAM

Just another four-letter word.
>TENNESSEE WILLIAMS

Love is the answer, but while you're waiting for the answer, sex raises some pretty good questions.
>WOODY ALLEN

To live is like to love – all reason is against it, and all healthy instinct for it.
>SAMUEL BUTLER
>*Note-Books*

Love, love, love – all the wretched cant of it, masking egotism, lust, masochism, fantasy under a mythology of sentimental postures, a welter of self-induced miseries and joys …
>GERMAINE GREER
>*The Female Eunuch*

Love affairs are the only real education in life.
>MARLENE DIETRICH

Love is a platform upon which all ranks meet.
>   W.S. GILBERT
>   *HMS Pinafore*

Love does not recognise the difference between peasant and mikado.
>   JAPANESE PROVERB

Love better is than Fame.
>   BAYARD TAYLOR
>   *To J.L.G.*

Love is like a wildflower that grows on the edge of a precipice, if you don't dare you don't touch it – and I'm glad we dared.
>   DAVID OWEN
>   in a letter to his wife Deborah quoted in his autobiography

What is love without passion? – A garden without flowers, a hat without feathers, tobogganing without snow.
>   JENNIE JEROME CHURCHILL
>   *His Borrowed Plumes*, 1909

Great passions don't exist, they are liar's fantasies. What do exist are little loves that may last for a short or longer while.
>   ANNA MAGNANI

Love is the fruit of idleness.
>   OLD ENGLISH PROVERB

Love is the egotism of two.
>   ANTOINE DE SALLE

A narcissism shared by two.
RITA MAE BROWN

Life has taught us that love does not consist in gazing at each other but in looking outward together in the same direction.
ANTOINE DE SAINT-EXUPERY
Airman's Odyssey

Love, the strongest and deepest element in all life, the harbinger of hope, of joy, of ecstasy; love, the defier of all laws, of all conventions; love, the freest, the most powerful moulder of human destiny; how can such an all-compelling force be synonymous with that poor little State and Church-begotten weed, marriage?
> EMMA GOLDMAN
> 'Marriage and Love', *Anarchism and Other Essays*, 1911

Marriage is law, and love is instinct.
> GUY DE MAUPASSANT
> *The Love of Long Ago*

Love is so much better when you are not married.
> MARIA CALLAS

Love is spontaneous. It surprises and invades; it never reasons; it has no need to interrogate itself, to surround itself with defences, plans of attack, and projects of retreat. It betrays itself, and then only is it restrained.
> GEORGE SAND

Love does not express itself on command; it cannot be called out like a dog to its master ... Love is autonomous; it obeys only itself.
> ROBERT C. MURPHY
> *Psychotherapy Based on Human Longing*

Love is the child of freedom, never that of domination.
> ERICH FROMM
> *The Art of Loving*

'Free love' – as if a lover ever had been or could be free.
> G.K. CHESTERTON
> *The Defendant*

Love will not be constrained by mastery;
When mastery comes, the god of love anon
Beats his fair wings, and farewell! He is gone!
Love is a thing as any spirit free;
Women by nature love their liberty,
And not to be constrained like any thrall,
And so do men, if say the truth I shall.
    GEOFFREY CHAUCER
    'The Franklin's Tale', *The Canterbury Tales*

The emotion, the ecstasy of love, we all want, but God spare us the responsibility.
    JESSAMYN WEST
    Love Is Not What You Think

Only by oneself, apart, can one consummate this seemingly most shared experience that love is.
    RAINER MARIA RILKE
    Letters

Love, n. The folly of thinking much of another before one knows anything of oneself.
>AMBROSE BIERCE
>*The Enlarged Devil's Dictionary*

I suppose love is whatever breaks and bridges the terrible pathos of separateness of human beings from each other. It doesn't mean much, however, unless it exists between two people who are uniquely themselves.
>MAX LERNER
>*The Unfinished Country*

Love is the irresistible desire to be irresistibly desired.
>ROBERT FROST

Most of us love from our need to love not because we find someone deserving.
>NIKKI GIOVANNI
>*The Women and the Men*

It is a name men and women are much in the habit of employing to sanctify their appetites.
>GEORGE MEREDITH
>*The Ordeal of Richard Feverel*

That what is commonly called love, namely, the desire of satisfying a voracious appetite with a certain quantity of delicate white human flesh …
>HENRY FIELDING
>*Tom Jones*

Sex is easy; it is love people ache for.
>JILL TWEEDIE
>*In the Name of Love*

Love is but the discovery of ourselves in others, and the delight in the recognition.
>   ALEXANDER SMITH
>   *Dreamthorp*

To be loved for what one is, is the greatest exception. The great majority love in another only what they lend him, their own selves, their version of him.
>   GOETHE
>   *Wisdom and Experience*

To be in love is merely to be in a state of perceptual anaesthesia – to mistake an ordinary young man for a Greek god or an ordinary young woman for a goddess.
>   H.L. MENCKEN
>   *Prejudices*

It's a drug. It distorts reality, and that's the point of it. It would be impossible to fall in love with someone that you really saw.
>   FRAN LEBOWITZ

Falling in love is the greatest imaginative experience of which most human beings are capable.
>   A.N. WILSON

Of Men and Women

Every man ought to be in love a few times in his life, and to have a smart attack of the fever. You are the better for it when it is over: the better for your misfortune if you endure it with a manly heart; how much the better for success if you win it and a good wife into the bargain!
W.M. THACKERAY
'Mr Brown's Letters to His Nephew'

There is always a woman chosen for a man; never does God create anyone without reserving his happiness in another being.
GEORGE SAND

A man sees beauty, or that which he likes, with eyes entirely his own. I don't say that plain women get husbands as readily as the pretty girls – but so many handsome girls are unmarried, and so many of the other sort wedded, that there is no possibility of establishing a rule ... Poor dear Mrs Brown was a far finer woman than Emily Blenkinsop, and yet I loved Emily's little finger more than the whole hand which your Aunt Martha gave me – I see the plainest women exercising the greatest fascinations over men – in fine, a man falls in love with a woman because it is fate, because she is a woman.
    W.M. THACKERAY
    'Mr Brown's Letters to His Nephew'

Speed: If you love her you cannot see her.
Valentine: Why?
Speed: Because Love is blind.
    WILLIAM SHAKESPEARE
    The Two Gentlemen of Verona

If Jack's in love, he's no judge of Jill's Beauty.
    BENJAMIN FRANKLIN
    Poor Richard

Many a man has fallen in love with a girl in a light so dim he would not have chosen a suit by it.
    MAURICE CHEVALIER

Blind love mistakes a harelip for a dimple.
    AMERICAN PROVERB

There is one woman whom fate has destined for each of us. If we miss her, we are saved.
    ANON

That gentlemen prefer blondes is due to the fact that, apparently, pale hair, delicate skin and an infantile expression represent the very apex of a frailty which every man longs to violate.
>   ALEXANDER KING
>   *Rich Man, Poor Man, Freud and Fruit*

People who are not in love cannot understand how an intelligent man can suffer because of a very ordinary woman. This is like being surprised that someone should be stricken with cholera because of something as insignificant as the common bacillus.
>   MARCEL PROUST

Love often makes a fool of the cleverest man, and as often gives cleverness to the most foolish.
>   OLD FRENCH PROVERB

It is as absurd to deny that it is possible for a man always to love the same woman, as it would be to claim that some famous musician needed several violins in order to execute a piece of music.
>   HONORÉ DE BALZAC
>   *Physiologie du mariage*

I've never been able to work without a woman to love. Perhaps I'm cruel. They are earth and sky and warmth and light to me. I'm like an Irish peasant, taking potatoes out of the ground. I live by the woman loved. I take from her. I know damned well I don't give enough.
>   SHERWOOD ANDERSON
>   in a letter

As soon as you cannot keep anything from a woman, you love her.
>   PAUL GÉRALDY

I lose my respect for the man who can make the mystery of sex the subject of a coarse jest, yet, when you speak earnestly and seriously on the subject, is silent.
>HENRY D. THOREAU
>*Journal*, 12 April 1852

A man may talk inspiringly to a woman about love in the abstract – but the look in his eyes is always perfectly concrete.
>HELEN ROWLAND

Men who do not make advances to women are apt to become victims to women who make advances to them.
>WALTER BAGEHOT
>*Biographical Studies*

>Man's love is of man's life a thing apart,
>'Tis woman's whole existence.
>>LORD BYRON
>>*Don Juan*

Love is the whole history of a woman's life; it is but an episode in a man's.
>   MADAME DE STAËL
>   *De l'Influence des passions*

Captain Harville smiled, as much as to say, 'Do you claim that for your sex?' and she answered the question, smiling also, 'Yes, we certainly do not forget you so soon as you forget us. It is, perhaps, our fate rather than our merit. We cannot help ourselves. We live at home, quiet, confined, and our feelings prey upon us. You are forced on exertion. You have always a profession, pursuits, business of some sort or other, to take you back into the world immediately, and continual occupation and change soon weaken impressions.' …

'No, no, it is not man's nature. I will not allow it to be more man's nature than woman's to be inconstant and forget those they do love, or have loved. I believe the reverse. I believe in a true analogy between our bodily frames and our mental; and that as our bodies are the strongest, so are our feelings; capable of bearing most rough usage, and riding out the heaviest weather.' …

'Oh!' cried Anne, eagerly … 'I should deserve utter contempt if I dared to suppose that true attachment and constancy were known only by woman. No, I believe you capable of everything great and good in your married lives. I believe you equal to every important exertion, and to every domestic forbearance, so long as – if I may be allowed the expression, so long as you have an object. I mean while the woman you love lives, and lives for you. All the privilege I claim for my own sex (it is not a very enviable one: you need not covet it), is that of loving longest, when existence or when hope is gone!'
>   JANE AUSTEN
>   *Persuasion*

When a woman likes to wait on a man, that settles it: she loves him.
E.W. HOWE
Country Town Sayings

Pride – that's a luxury a woman in love can't afford.
CLARE BOOTHE LUCE

No woman ever loved her husband for his intellect or his admirable principles – ... *love is the instinctive movement of personality.*
J.B. YEATS
Letters to His Son, W.B. Yeats, and Others

Love is not getting, but giving. It is sacrifice. And sacrifice is glorious! I have no patience with women who measure and weigh their love like a country doctor dispensing capsules. If a man is worth loving at all, he is worth loving generously, even recklessly.
MARIE DRESSLER
My Own Story, 1934

Love is always the soul of every conversation in which women take part.
GEORGE SAND

Men are often blind to the passions of women; but every woman is as quick-sighted as a hawk on these occasions.
HENRY FIELDING
Amelia

A lady's imagination is very rapid; it jumps from admiration to love, from love to matrimony in a moment.
JANE AUSTEN
Pride and Prejudice

No woman marries for money; they are all clever enough, before marrying a millionaire, to fall in love with him first.
CESARE PAVESE

With every woman, to love a man is to feel that she must positively know just where is going as soon as he is out of her sight.
F. MARION CRAWFORD

… that sex without which man would be the most miserable animal on earth.
GIACOMO CASANOVA
Memoirs

Of True Love

When the satisfaction or security of another person becomes as significant to one as is one's own satisfaction or security, then the state of love exists.
> HARRY STACK SULLIVAN
> *Conceptions of Modern Psychiatry*

True love shows, when it is there; it cannot dissemble.
> CHRISTINE DE PISAN
> 'The Epistle of Othea to Hector'

All true love is grounded on esteem.
> GEORGE VILLIERS, DUKE OF BUCKINGHAM

By every inch we grow in intellectual height our love strikes down its roots deeper, and spreads out its arms wider.
> OLIVE SCHREINER
> *The Story of an African Farm*, 1883

Two persons love in one another the future good which they aid one another to unfold.
MARGARET FULLER
American feminist, writing in *The Dial*, 1843

Love disregards manifest qualities and sees right through them down to the true essential value. Furthermore, love divines all the talents, the still dormant possibilities of the beloved, brings them to life, and thus increases his value.
OSWALD SCHWARZ
The Psychology of Sex

To be capable of giving and receiving mature love is as sound a criterion as we have for the fulfilled personality. But by that very token it is a goal gained only in proportion to how much one has fulfilled the prior condition of becoming a personality in one's own right.
ROLLO MAY
Man's Search for Himself

The curious point is that the more profound our love is the less we are conscious of it as love ... Consciousness of love, like all other consciousness, vanishes on becoming intense. While we are yet fully aware of it, we do not love as well as we think we do.
SAMUEL BUTLER
Note-Books

Love is not getting, but giving; not a wild dream of pleasure, and a madness of desire – oh, no, love is not that – it is goodness, and honor, and peace and pure living.
HENRY VAN DYKE
Little Rivers: A Handful of Heather

Of all the realities whose values we ignore, in childish preoccupation with our feeble dreams, the human realities of companionship which each sex has to offer the other are among the richest. Despite all our romantic serenadings, men and women have only begun to discover each other.
FLOYD DELL
Were You Ever a Child?

Love's Endurance

'Oh Jack, this is delightful! If you'll only keep up the pace, I'm sure I shall soon gain confidence.' Jack has already run a mile, and is very out of condition. From *Punch* in 1896.

First Love

Children do fall in love even though their elders do not take them seriously.
　　JOHN ERSKINE
　　The Complete Life

Ah, how I loved her! What happiness (I thought) if we were married, and were going away anywhere to love among the trees and in the fields, never growing older, never growing wiser, children ever, rambling hand in hand through sunshine and among flowery meadows, laying down our heads on moss at night, in a sweet sleep of purity and peace ... Some such picture, with no real world in it, bright with the light of our innocence, and vague as the stars afar off, was in my mind all the way. I am glad to think there were two such guileless hearts at Peggotty's marriage as Little Em'ly's and mine.
　　CHARLES DICKENS
　　David Copperfield

Pandora and I are in love! It is official! She told Claire Neilson, who told Nigel, who told me.
>   SUE TOWNSEND
>   *The Secret Diary of Adrian Mole Aged 13¾*

Rosie told me outrageous fantasies. She liked me, she said, better than Walt, or Ken, Boney Harris, or even the curate. And I admitted to her, in a loud, rough voice, that she was even prettier than Betty Gleed.
>   LAURIE LEE
>   *Cider with Rosie*

'Say, Becky, was you ever engaged?'

'What's that?'

'Why, engaged to be married.'

'No.'

'Would you like to?'

'I reckon so. I don't know. What is it like?'

'Like? Why, it ain't like anything. You only just tell a boy you won't ever have anybody but him, ever ever *ever*, and then you kiss, and that's all. Anybody can do it.'
>   MARK TWAIN
>   *The Adventures of Tom Sawyer*

'*Loving!*' cried I, as scornfully as I could utter the word. '*Loving!*' Did anybody ever hear the like! I might just as well talk of loving the miller who comes once a year to buy our corn. Pretty loving, indeed! and both times together you have seen Linton hardly four hours in your life!'
>   EMILY BRONTË
>   Nelly Dean reproves young Catherine,
>   *Wuthering Heights*

A boy's love comes from a full heart; a man's is more often the result of a full stomach. Indeed a man's sluggish current may not be called love, compared with the rushing fountain that wells up, when a boy's heart is struck with the heavenly rod. If you would taste love, drink of the pure stream that youth pours out at your feet. Do not wait till it has become a muddy river.
>   JEROME K. JEROME
>   *The Idle Thoughts of an Idle Fellow*

'What are you doing sitting on that wall?' Zinaida asked me, with a strange smile on her face, and she went on, 'You are always telling me you love me – well if you do, you can jump down on to the road.'

She had barely finished speaking before I jumped, as though someone had pushed me from behind. The wall was a high one. I landed on my feet but the impact was so strong that I was unable to keep upright; I fell, and for a moment lost consciousness. When I came to, I could feel, without opening my eyes, that Zinaida was close.

'My darling boy,' she murmured, bending over me, and her voice sounded alarmed and tender, 'how could you do such a thing, how could you listen … truly I love you …'

I could feel her chest near mine as her hands cupped my head, and suddenly – imagine my delight – her soft, fresh lips started to cover my whole face with kisses …

But then Zinaida probably guessed, from the expression on my face, that I had regained consciousness, although I still kept my eyes shut, and quickly rose …

The bliss I experienced then has never been repeated in all my life.
>   IVAN TURGENEV
>   *First Love*

We were so unrestrained in our caresses that we could not even wait to be alone. The postilions and the innkeepers along the road looked on with admiration, and I could see they were surprised that two youngsters of our age appeared to love one another with such frenzy. Our intention to get married was forgotten at Saint-Denis.
　　ABBÉ PRÉVOST
　　Manon Lescaut

'It all happens in a flash,' Jenny said. 'It happened to Teenie when she was out walking at Puddocky with her boy friend. Then they had to get married.'
　　MURIEL SPARK
　　The Prime of Miss Jean Brodie

> I ne'er was struck before that hour
> With love so sudden and so sweet.
> Her face it bloomed like a sweet flower
> And stole my heart away complete.
> My face turned pale as deadly pale,
> My legs refused to walk away;
> And when she looked 'what could I ail?'
> My life and all seemed turned to clay.
>> JOHN CLARE
>> 'First Love'

To fall in love you have to be in the state of mind for it to take, like a disease.
> NANCY MITFORD

It was as if he had seen a vision. She was sitting on the bench, alone, or at least he did not notice any one else, so dazzled was he by the sight of her …

She was wearing a large straw hat, with pink ribbons which fluttered behind her in the breeze. Her dark hair was divided into bandeaux which framed her oval face … What was her name, where did she live, what sort of life did she lead, what was her past? He wanted to know how her bedroom was furnished, all the dresses she had ever worn, the people she saw; and the desire of physical possession was subsumed by a deeper felt desire, and by a painful and limitless curiosity.
> GUSTAVE FLAUBERT
> *L'Education sentimentale*
> the start for Frédéric of a lifelong passion for Madame Arnoux

Love can hope where reason would despair.
> GEORGE LYTTELTON
> 'Epigram'

John waited, taking in with all his soul Elizabeth as she stood, a dark cloak now over her shoulders; the rest of the world, the dancers, the lighted fires, the stars that sparkled above the heavy wood, vanished. She was alone and in her silence and quiet a saint in a chapel secret and remote for his own single worship. He stayed there a long while. In his twenty years he had known no feeling like this, nothing that made him both so proud and so humble, so resolute and so brave, but so timid also with a shy foreboding.

She was a child, eight years younger than himself; she was the daughter of his greatest enemy.
    HUGH WALPOLE
    The Herries Chronicle

If it is your time love will track you down like a cruise missile. If you say 'No! I don't want it right now', that's when you'll get it for sure.
    LYNDA BARRY
    Big Ideas

Not only was he tall and attractive, but he also carried not one unnecessary ounce on his hard masculine body, as was made obvious by his thin cotton shirt open nearly to the waist and tucked inside a distressingly tight pair of jeans.
    JOY HOWARD
    Stormy Paradise

… love's true arrow …
    JOHN CLELAND
    Fanny Hill

Love at first sight is cured by a second look.
    AMERICAN PROVERB

To-day I fell in love with Fanny Thomas.

I danced the first quadrille with her and made innumerable mistakes, once or twice running quite wild through the figure like a runaway horse, but she was so goodhumoured and longsuffering. It was a very happy evening. How little I knew what was in store for me when I came to Llan Thomas this afternoon.
>   REVD FRANCIS KILVERT
>   *Diary*, 8 September 1871

It is difficult to know at what moment love begins; it is less difficult to know that it has begun.
>   HENRY WADSWORTH LONGFELLOW
>   *Hyperion*

I don't remember who was there, except Dora. I have not the least idea what we had for dinner, besides Dora. My impression is, that I dined off Dora entirely, and sent away half-a-dozen plates untouched. I sat next to her. I talked to her. She had the most delightful little voice, the gayest little laugh, the pleasantest and most fascinating little ways, that ever led a lost youth into hopeless slavery.
>   CHARLES DICKENS
>   *David Copperfield*

He gave her a look you could have poured on a waffle.
>   RING GARDNER

Lying in bed this morning dozing, half awake and half asleep, I composed my speech of thanks at my wedding breakfast, a very affecting speech, and had visions of myself with Daisy at Langley and other places.
>   REVD FRANCIS KILVERT
>   *Diary*, 15 September 1871

Love detects nuances which are invisible to indifferent eyes, and draws endless conclusions from them.
>   STENDHAL
>   *La Chartreuse de Parme*

Clelia came to her window two or three times a day to inspect her bird cages, sometimes for a few moments only. If Fabrice had not been so much in love, he would have realized that she loved him; but as it was he had terrible doubts on the matter.

Clelia had had a piano placed in front of the window, so that her presence there was accounted for by the sentinels who walked along the rampart below. As she played, she sought to reply with her eyes to Fabrice's questions.

And so, although confined to a rather small cell, Fabrice led a very busy life: his time was entirely taken up by seeking the solution to the all important question of whether she loved him.
>   STENDHAL
>   *La Chartreuse de Parme*

… those tender doubts which are almost inseparable from Love.
>   ELIZA HAYWOOD
>   *The Secret History of the Present Intrigues of the Court of Caramania*

Love is so very timid when 'tis new.
>   LORD BYRON
>   *Don Juan*

Nowadays … it's 'darling' and 'come to my place' in the first hour.
>   MARYA MANNES
>   *Life*, 12 June 1964

No sooner met, but they looked; no sooner looked, but they loved; no sooner loved, but they sighed; no sooner sighed, but they asked one another the reason.
WILLIAM SHAKESPEARE

I can see from your utter misery, from your eagerness to misunderstand each other, and from your thoroughly bad temper that this is the real thing.
PETER USTINOV
in the film *Romanoff and Juliet*, 1957

... the delights and tortures, the jealousy and wakefulness, the longing and raptures, the frantic despair and elation, attendant upon the passion of love.
W.M. THACKERAY
'Mr Brown's Letters to His Nephew'

Those early days of love and passion are extraordinary. I feel sorry for anyone who's never experienced them. And it can go on, and on, it's nothing to do with age.
HELEN MIRREN
in a *Times* interview, March 1994

The magic of first love is our ignorance that it can ever end.
BENJAMIN DISRAELI

You've been in love, of course! If not you've got it to come. Love is like the measles; we all have to go through it. Also like the measles, we take it only once. One never need be afraid of catching it a second time … Cupid spends no second arrow on the same heart … We like, we cherish, we are very, very fond – but we never love again. A man's heart is a firework that once in its time flashes heavenward. Meteor-like, it blazes for a moment, and lights with its glory the whole world beneath.
JEROME K. JEROME
The Idle Thoughts of an Idle Fellow

Declarations

'In vain have I struggled. It will not do. My feelings will not be repressed. You must allow me to tell you how ardently I admire and love you.'

Elizabeth's astonishment was beyond expression. She stared, coloured, doubted, and was silent. This he considered sufficient encouragement; and the avowal of all that he felt, and had long felt for her, immediately followed.
JANE AUSTEN
Pride and Prejudice

Coningsby ... had seated himself on a log almost at her feet. And assuredly a maiden and a youth more beautiful and engaging had seldom met before in a scene more fresh and fair. Edith on her rustic seat watched the now blue and foaming river, and the birch-trees with a livelier tint, and quivering in the sunset air; an expression of tranquil bliss suffused her beautiful brow, and spoke from the thrilling tenderness of her soft dark eye. Coningsby gazed on that countenance with a glance of entranced rapture. His cheek was flushed, his eye gleamed with dazzling lustre. She turned her head, she met that glance, and, troubled, she withdrew her own.

'Edith!' he said in a tone of tremulous passion, 'Let me call you Edith! Yes,' he continued, gently taking her hand, 'let me call you my Edith! I love you!'

She did not withdraw her hand; but turned away a face flushed as the impending twilight.
BENJAMIN DISRAELI
Coningsby

At last I couldn't bear it any longer, and after I had walked up and down the sunny side of Oxford Street in tight boots for a week – and a devilish hot summer it was too – in the hope of meeting her, I sat down and wrote a letter, and begged her to manage to see me clandestinely, for I wanted to hear her decision from her own mouth. I said I had discovered, to my perfect satisfaction, that I couldn't live without her, and that if she didn't have me, I had made up my mind to take prussic acid, or take to drinking, or emigrate, so as to take myself off in some way or other.
>   CHARLES DICKENS
>   Mr Parsons describes his suffering, *Sketches by Boz*

Nobody in love has a sense of humour.
>   S.N. BEHRMAN
>   *The Second Man*

I love you more than a wasp can sting,
And more than the subway jerks,
I love you as much as a beggar needs a crutch,
And more than a hangnail irks.
>   OGDEN NASH
>   'To My Valentine'

You are more than a jar full of sticklebacks and a bag full of conkers.
>   Valentine message in *The Times*, February 1994

I love thee like pudding; if thou wert pie, I'd eat thee.
>   JOHN RAY

Darling Honey-pig. Be my Valentine truffle? All my love. Piglet.
>   Valentine message in *The Times*, February 1994

'I am able now to ease my bosom of a heavy load, and speak to you in confidence. Mary,' said Mr Pecksniff in his tenderest tones: indeed, they were so very tender that he almost squeaked 'My soul! I love you!'

A fantastic thing, that maiden affectation! She made believe to shudder.

'I love you,' said Mr Pecksniff, 'my gentle life, with a devotion which is quite surprising, even to myself ...'

She tried to disengage her hand, but might as well have tried to free herself from the embrace of an affectionate boa-constrictor.
    CHARLES DICKENS
    Martin Chuzzlewit

Then, having me in his arms, he kissed me three or four times. I struggled to get away, and yet did it but faintly neither, and he held me fast, and still kissed me, till he was out of breath, and sitting down, says he, 'Dear Betty, I am in love with you.'

His words, I must confess, fired my blood; all my spirits flew about my heart, and put me into disorder enough. He repeated it afterwards several times, that he was in love with me, and my heart spoke as plain as a voice that I liked it.
    DANIEL DEFOE
    Moll Flanders

If a young woman once thinks herself handsome, she never doubts the truth of any man that tells her he is in love with her; for if she believes herself charming enough to captivate him, 'tis natural to expect the effects of it.
    DANIEL DEFOE
    Moll Flanders

To live without seeing you everyday would be a far worse ordeal than being in this prison! I have never been so happy in my life! Is it not a delicious irony that I have found happiness in prison?
>STENDHAL
>Fabrice to Clelia, the gaoler's daughter
>*La Chartreuse de Parme*

'I could be happy with her,' cried he, convulsively, 'in a hovel! I could go down with her into poverty and the dust!'
>WASHINGTON IRVING
>*The Sketch Book of Geoffrey Crayon, Gent*

'I should not have believed any one who told me that I was capable of such love,' said Prince Andrew. 'It is not at all the same feeling that I knew in the past. The whole world is now for me divided into two halves: one half is Natasha, and there is all joy, hope and light; the other half is everything else, and there all is darkness and gloom …'
>LEO TOLSTOY
>*War and Peace*

I can listen no longer in silence. I must speak to you by such means as are within my reach. You pierce my soul. I am half agony, half hope. Tell me not that I am too late, that such precious feelings are gone for ever. I offer myself to you again with a heart even more your own than when you almost broke it, eight years and a half ago. Dare not say that man forgets sooner than woman, that his love has an earlier death. I have loved none but you. Unjust I may have been, weak and resentful I have been, but never inconstant.
>JANE AUSTEN
>Captain Wentworth writes to Anne
>*Persuasion*

Any man's nice when he's in love.
>   HENRY JAMES
>   *The Ambassadors*

'Tis not your saying that you love,
Can ease me of my smart;
Your actions must your words approve,
Or else you break my heart.
>   APHRA BEHN
>   'Song'

Fall at the feet of your idol as you wish, but drag her down to your level after that.
>   BARONESS ORCZY
>   *I Will Repay*

They were such strangers. Only, of course, strangers on the lower level of everyday circumstances. On the higher level, the starry level of splendid, unreasoning love, he had, as he told her, always known her.
ELIZABETH VON ARNIM
Love

Love creates, as though by magic, a past with which it surrounds us. It gives us, so to speak, the feeling that we have lived for years, with a being who previously was practically a stranger to us. Love is but a luminous point, and yet it seems to take hold of time.
BENJAMIN CONSTANT
Adolphe

Lucy was very inquisitive about everything and everybody at Raynham. Whoever had been about Richard since his birth, she must know the history of, and he for a kiss will do her bidding.
GEORGE MEREDITH
The Ordeal of Richard Feverel

The day was about to die; the day the most important, the most precious in the lives of Harry Coningsby and Edith Millbank. Words had been spoken, vows breathed, which were to influence their careers for ever. For them hereafter there was to be but one life, one destiny, one world. Each of them was still in such a state of tremulous excitement, that neither had found time or occasion to ponder over the mighty result. They both required solitude; they both longed to be alone.
BENJAMIN DISRAELI
Coningsby

My love for Linton is like the foliage in the woods: time will change it, I'm well aware, as winter changes the trees. My love for Heathcliff resembles the eternal rocks beneath: a source of little visible delight, but necessary. Nelly, I *am* Heathcliff.
    EMILY BRONTE
    Wuthering Heights

I have fallen in love with Alfred de Musset, and this time it is very serious indeed. It is no caprice but steadfast devotion ... I cannot predict whether this affection will last long enough to make it in your eyes as sacred as the affections to which you are liable. I once loved for six years, another time for three, and this time round I am unable to say how long it will last.
    GEORGE SAND
    in a letter to her friend, the critic Sainte-Beuve,
    in May 1832

I swear to you that never does your image leave me, night or day, even in the midst of business. My love is a constant sensation which nothing interrupts, which alternates between absolute and tender devotion and acute agony ... Oh, if you loved me as I love you, what happiness would we not enjoy!
    BENJAMIN CONSTANT
    in a letter to the society beauty Juliette
    Récamier, January 1815

Romeo writes to you, Juliette ... O Juliette, life without love is but a long sleep; the most beautiful of women must surely have feelings – happy the mortal who will become the friend of your heart ...
    LUCIEN BONAPARTE
    in a letter to Juliette Récamier, 27 July 1799.
    But he retired after a year's courtship.

You fear, sometimes, I do not love you so much as you wish? My dear Girl I love you ever and ever and without reserve. The more I have known you the more have I lov'd ... You are always new. The last of your kisses was ever the sweetest; the last smile the brightest; the last movement the gracefullest. When you pass'd my window home yesterday, I was fill'd with as much admiration as if I had then seen you for the first time ... Even if you did not love me I could not help an entire devotion to you: how much more deeply then must I feel for you knowing you love me.
>
> JOHN KEATS
> in a letter to Fanny Brawne, *c*. March 1820

In that word, beautiful in all languages, but most so in yours – *Amor mio* – is comprised my existence here and hereafter – to *what* purpose you will decide; my destiny rests with you, and you are a woman, eighteen years of age, and two out of a convent. I wish that you had stayed there, with all my heart – or, at least, that I had never met you in your married state.

But all this is too late. I love you, and you love me – at least, you *say so*, and *act* as if you *did* so, which last is a great consolation in all events. But *I* more than love you, and cannot cease to love you.

Think of me, sometimes, when the Alps and ocean divide us – but they never will, unless you *wish* it.
>
> LORD BYRON
> in a letter to Teresa Guiccioli, 25 August 1819,
> from Bologna

Oceans: A minute measure of Love.
>
> OLIVER HERFORD
> *Cupid's Cyclopedia*, 1910

It is the hardest thing in the world to be in love and yet attend to business. As for me, all who speak to me find me out, and I must lock myself up or other people will do it for me.

A gentleman asked me this morning, 'What news from Lisbon?' and I answered, 'She is exquisitely handsome.' ... O love! –

'A thousand torments dwell about me!

Yet who would live to live without thee?'

Methinks I could write a volume to you; but all the language on earth would fail in saying how much and with what disinterested passion I am ever yours.
    RICHARD STEELE
    in a letter to Mary Scurlock in August 1707

  O, Love, love, love!
  Love is like a dizziness;
  It winna let a poor body
  Gang about his biziness!
    JAMES HOGG

Ask me no reason why I love you; for though Love use reason for his physician, he admits him not for his counsellor. You are not young, no more am I; go to then, there's sympathy; you are merry, so am I – ha! ha! then there's more sympathy; you love sack and so do I; would you desire better sympathy? Let it suffice thee, Mistress Page – at the least if the love of a soldier can suffice – that I love thee. I will not say pity me; 'tis not a soldier-like phrase; but I say, love me ...
    WILLIAM SHAKESPEARE
    Sir John Falstaff's letter to Mistress Page,
    The Merry Wives of Windsor

I love you, my poor angel, you know that perfectly well, and yet you want me to put it in writing …
VICTOR HUGO
in a letter to Juliette Drouet, 7 March 1833

I am a stranger in these matters E[llison], as I assure you, that you are the first woman to whom I ever made such a declaration so I declare I am at a loss how to proceed.
ROBERT BURNS
in a letter to Ellison Begbie, 1781

I never had the least thought or inclination of turning Poet till I got heartily in Love, and then Rhyme and Song were, in a manner, the spontaneous language of my heart.
ROBERT BURNS
First Commonplace Book, August 1783

O, my luve's like a red, red rose,
That's newly sprung in June:
O, my luve's like the melodie
That's sweetly played in tune.

As fair art thou, my bonnie lass,
So deep in luve am I;
And I will luve thee still, my dear,
Till a' the seas gang dry.
ROBERT BURNS
'A Red, Red Rose'

I am two fooles, I know,
For loving, and for saying so
In whining Poetry …
JOHN DONNE
'The Triple Foole'

How do I love thee? Let me count the ways.
I love thee to the depth and breadth and height
My soul can reach ...
>ELIZABETH BARRETT BROWNING
>'Sonnets from the Portuguese', the sequence of personal poems written before her marriage

My bounty is as boundless as the sea,
My love as deep, the more I give to thee
The more I have, for both are infinite.
>WILLIAM SHAKESPEARE
>Juliet's goodnight, *Romeo and Juliet*

Our love is an eternal thing, like the sea and the wind.
>HAROLD NICOLSON
>in a letter to Vita Sackville-West

Love has a tide!
>HELEN HUNT JACKSON
>'Tides'

What would I not do for love of you, my own Clara! The knights of old were better off; they could go through fire or slay dragons to win their ladies, but we of today have to content ourselves with more prosaic methods, such as smoking fewer cigars, and the like.
>ROBERT SCHUMANN
>in a letter to Clara Wieck, 2 January 1838

Think you, if Laura had been Petrarch's wife,
He would have written sonnets all his life?
>LORD BYRON
>*Don Juan*

Love everywhere tends to magnify both its object and itself. It makes unreasonable claims as to its own strength, depth, duration, and intensity.
OSCAR W. FIRKINS
in a letter

Will you love me in December as you do in May,
Will you love me in the good old fashioned way?
When my hair has all turned grey,
Will you kiss me then and say,
That you love me in December as you do in May?
JAMES J. WALKER
popular song, 1905

Kisses

Kiss: A course of procedure, cunningly devised, for the mutual stoppage of speech at a moment when words are superfluous.
>OLIVER HERFORD
>*Cupid's Cyclopedia*, 1910

The sound of a kiss is not so loud as that of a cannon, but its echo lasts a great deal longer.
>OLIVER WENDELL HOLMES

First Kiss: Much has been written about the exquisite joy of this, still it is unsatisfying, hence the Second, the Third, etc, *ad lib*.
>OLIVER HERFORD
>*Cupid's Cyclopedia*, 1910

To a woman the first kiss is the end of the beginning; to a man it is the beginning of the end.
>HELEN ROWLAND

His large, glittering, masculine eyes were so close to hers that she saw nothing but them.

'Natalie?' he whispered inquiringly while she felt her hands being painfully pressed. 'Natalie?' ...

Burning lips were pressed to hers.
>   LEO TOLSTOY
>   *War and Peace*

Benjie took her in his arms and kissed her with a ferocity that Ouida – a novel by whom Vanessa had recently been enjoying describes somewhere 'as the lovely tiger's grandeur and the abandoned wildness of the jungle' ... This was the first time in her life that Vanessa had ever been passionately kissed. She found it entrancing.
>   HUGH WALPOLE
>   *The Herries Chronicle*

As we were sitting together, suddenly there came into her eyes a look that I had never seen there before. My lips moved towards hers. We kissed each other. I can't describe to you what I felt at that moment. It seemed to me that all my life had been narrowed to one perfect point of rose-coloured joy. She trembled all over, and shook like a white narcissus.
>OSCAR WILDE
>*The Picture of Dorian Gray*

'How can I prove it more than I have done?' she cried, in a distraction of tenderness. 'Will this prove it more?'

She clasped his neck, and for the first time Clare learnt what an impassioned woman's kisses were like upon the lips of one whom she loved with all her heart and soul, as Tess loved him.
>THOMAS HARDY
>*Tess of the d'Urbervilles*

Kissing a man without a mustache is like eating an egg without salt.
>RUDYARD KIPLING

Oh, what a dear, ravishing thing is the beginning of an amour!
APHRA BEHN

Knee: An adjustable, animated settee designed for the use of ladies.
OLIVER HERFORD
Cupid's Cyclopedia

But his kiss was so sweet, and so closely he pressed, that I languished and pined till I granted the rest.
JOHN GAY

Darling Poochi Woochi!! Huggy wuggy, Kissie Wissie, Nozzle Bozzle, Nauti Pawti!!
Valentine message in *The Times*,
February 1993

Frequent kisses end in a baby.
HUNGARIAN PROVERB

Happy Days

Such a happy day. Thank God for such a happy day. I have seen my love, my own, I have seen Daisy. She was so lovely and sweet and kind and the old beautiful love is as fresh and strong as ever. I never saw her more happy and affectionate and her lovely Welsh eyes grew radiant whenever they met mine. She was looking prettier than ever and the East wind had freshened her pretty colour and her lovely hair was shining like gold. She wore a brown stuff dress and white ribbons in her hat.

I wonder if Daisy and I will ever read these pages over together. I think we shall.
REVD FRANCIS KILVERT
Diary, 6 November 1871

My heart is like a singing bird
Whose nest is in a water'd shoot;
My heart is like an apple tree
Whose boughs are bent with thick-set fruit;
My heart is like a rainbow shell
That paddles in a halcyon sea;
My heart is gladder than all these,
Because my love is come to me.
CHRISTINA ROSSETTI
'A Birthday'

She flowered in his warmth into a beauty she had never possessed in the tepid days of George. Obviously what the world needed was love.
ELIZABETH VON ARNIM
Love

Love has always been associated, quite rightly, with the countryside: there is no better setting for the woman one loves than a blue sky, sweet smells, flowers, breezes, the resplendent solitude of fields and woods.
    ALEXANDRE DUMAS
    La Dame aux camélias

Obstacles

A letter came from Mr Thomas. Kindly expressed and cordial, but bidding me give up all thoughts and hopes of Daisy. It was a great and sudden blow and I felt very sad. The sun seemed to have gone out of the sky. I wrote a courteous reply saying that I must abide by his decision, but that an attachment would not be worthy of the name which could be blown out by the first breath of difficulty and discouragement and that I should be more unworthy of his daughter than I was if I could give her up so lightly and easily.
    REVD FRANCIS KILVERT
    Diary, 23 September 1871

Young love needs dangers and barriers to nourish it.
    GEORGE SAND

'Yes, sir, it is in vain to speak of the enmities that are fostered between you and my grandfather; the love that exists between your daughter and myself is stronger than all your hatreds.'

    'You speak like a young man, and a young man that is in love,' said Mr Millbank. 'This is mere rhapsody; it will vanish in an instant before the reality of life.'
    BENJAMIN DISRAELI
    Coningsby

    For each ecstatic instant
    We must an anguish pay
    In keen and quivering ratio
    To the ecstasy …
        EMILY DICKINSON

My interview with your father was terrible. He was frigid, hostile, confused and contradictory at once ...

I feel so lifeless, so *humiliated*, today that I am incapable of a single fine thought. Even your picture is so blurred that I almost forget what your eyes are like. I am not so reduced in spirit as to think of giving you up, but so embittered by this outrage to my most sacred feelings, by being treated like one of the common herd ... To think that I am not allowed to see you! He will only allow it in some public place, where we should be a laughing-stock for everybody.
>   ROBERT SCHUMANN
>   in a letter to Clara Wieck, 18 September 1837

As is usual with most lovers in the city, they were troubled by the lack of that essential need of love – a meeting place.
>   THOMAS WOLFE
>   *The Web and the Rock*

Jul. The orchard walls are high and hard to climb,
     And the place death, considering who thou art,
     If any of my kinsmen find thee there.
Rom. With love's light wings did I o'er-perch these walls;
     For stony limits cannot hold love out,
     And what love can do that dares love attempt;
     Therefore thy kinsmen are no stop to me.
     WILLIAM SHAKESPEARE
     Romeo and Juliet

'I'm tied hand and foot, Matt. There isn't a thing I can do,' he began again.
  'You must write to me sometimes, Ethan.'

'Oh, what good'll writing do? I want to put my hand out and touch you. I want to do for you and care for you. I want to be there when you're sick and when you're lonesome.'
EDITH WHARTON
Ethan Frome

Doubt is in itself faithlessness; trust, the half of possession. We may leave the rest to our guardian angel, who destined us each for the other in our cradles.
ROBERT SCHUMANN
in a letter to Clara Wieck, 8 November 1837

Who can love without an anxious heart? How shall there be joy at meeting, without tears at parting?
W.M. THACKERAY
Rebecca and Rowena

Separation

Absence: A powerful stimulant to love. See *longing*.
　　OLIVER HERFORD
　　Cupid's Cyclopedia, 1910

'Writing to each other,' said Lucy, returning the letter into her pocket, 'is the only comfort we have in such long separations. Yes, I have one other comfort in his picture; but poor Edward has not even *that*. If he had but my picture, he says he should be easy. I gave him a lock of my hair set in a ring when he was at Longstaple last, and that was some comfort to him, he said, but not equal to a picture.'
　　JANE AUSTEN
　　Sense and Sensibility

What cannot letters inspire? They have souls; they can speak; they have in them all that force which expresses the transports of the heart; they have all the fire of our passions. They can rouse them as much as if the persons themselves were present. They have all the tenderness and the delicacy of speech, and sometimes even a boldness of expression beyond it.

HELOISE
in a letter to Abelard

'Tis but an howr since you went, and I am writeing to you already, is not this kinde? How doe you after your Journy? are you not weary? doe you not repent that you tooke it, to soe litle purpose? ...

Lord, there were a thousand things I rememberd after you were gon that I should have sayed, and now I am to write, not one of them will come into my head ... Good God, the fear's and surprizes, the crosses and disorders of that day, twas confused enough to bee a dream and I am apt to think somtimes it was noe more. but noe I saw you, when I shall doe it againe god only know's; can there bee a more Romance story then ours would make if the conclusion should prove happy?

DOROTHY OSBORNE
in a letter to William Temple, 13 January 1653/4

My dearest life

Having declared how delightfull this is to me, I hope it will not be unpleasant to you; tho' I have no more to say than what I have a thousand times told you, that I am yours with a most intire affection. How shall I tell you how ye time passes with me when I am from you; why truly ye night is to me as welcome as ye day, my thoughts are my only recreations, and these ye darkness hinders not; when that comes, tho' I sleep not, yet I do not complain; I love you no common way, for I shoud account it so much time lost, shoud not a kind dream represent you to me.

    THOMAS HERVEY
    in a letter during his long courtship of Isabella,
    whom he finally married in 1658, to enjoy 28
    happy years
    The Letter-Books of John Hervey

It is astonishing how much the state of the body influences the powers of the mind. I have been thinking all the morning of a very delightful and interesting letter I would send you this evening, and now I am so tired, and yet have so much to do, that my thoughts are quite giddy, and run round your image without any power of themselves to stop and admire it. I want to say a thousand kind and, believe me, heartfelt things to you, but am not master of words fit for the purpose; and still, as I ponder and think on you, chlorides, trials, oil, Davy, steel, miscellanea, mercury, and fifty other professional fancies swim before and drive me further and further into the quandary of stupidness.

    MICHAEL FARADAY
    in a letter to Sarah Barnard, December 1820.
    They did in fact marry shortly afterwards, and
    lived happily ever after.

My mistress and friend – My heart and I surrender ourselves into your hands, beseeching you to hold us commended to your favour, and that by absence your affection to us may not be lessened; for it would be a great pity to increase our pain, of which absence produces enough and more than I could ever have thought could be felt; reminding us of a point of astronomy which is this, – the longer the days are, the most distant is the sun, and nevertheless the hotter; so it is with our love, for by absence we are kept at a distance from one another, and yet it retains its fervour at least on my side. I hope the like on yours, assuring you that on my part the pain of absence is already too great for me; and when I think of the increase of that which I am forced to suffer, it would be almost intolerable but for the firm hope I have of your unchangeable affection for me.
    KING HENRY VIII
    in a letter to Anne Boleyn in 1528

My dearest Emma
… All your letters, *my dear letters*, are so entertaining, and which point so clearly what you are after that they give me either the greatest pleasure or pain. It is the next best thing to being with you.

I only desire, my dearest Emma, that you will always believe that Nelson's your own; Nelson's Alpha and Omega is Emma! I cannot alter – my affection and love is beyond even this world! Nothing will shake it but yourself, and that I will not allow myself to think for a moment is possible …

I rejoice that you have had so pleasant a trip into Norfolk, and I hope one day to carry you there by a nearer *tie* in law, but not in love and affection than at present …
    HORATIO NELSON
    in a letter to Emma Lady Hamilton, 26 August 1803

Unto my right well-beloved Valentine, John Paston, Esquire, be this bill delivered.

Right reverend and worshipful, and my right well-beloved Valentine, I recommend me unto you, full heartily desiring to hear of your welfare, which I beseech Almighty God long for to preserve unto His pleasure and your heart's desire.

And if it please you to hear of my welfare, I am not in good health of body nor of heart, nor shall be till I hear from you.

> MARGERY BREWS
> *The Paston Letters*, February 1477

I should like to call you by all the endearing epithets, and yet I can find no lovelier word than the simple word 'dear', but there is a particular way of saying it. My dear one, then, I have wept for joy to think that you are mine.

> ROBERT SCHUMANN
> in a letter to Clara Wieck, 2 January 1838

Send me the words 'Good night' to put under my pillow.

> JOHN KEATS
> in a letter to Fanny Brawne, February 1820

… wishing my self (specially an Evening) in my Sweethearts Armes whose pretty Duckys [breasts] I trust shortly to kysse. Written with the Hand of him that was, is, and shall be yours by his will.

> KING HENRY VIII
> in a letter to Anne Boleyn in 1528

Love Letters are effusions little suited to the public eye.

> THOMAS MOORE
> *Life of Byron*

As for my letters, I will deposit them with yours (for I have preserved every line that I ever received from you). There is nothing in them which may not be seen by men and angels, and though written, as their utter carelessness and unreserve may show, without the slightest reference to any other eyes than those to which they were addressed, I shall not be unwilling to think that when time has consecrated both our memories (which it will do), this correspondence may see the light.
ROBERT SOUTHEY
in a letter to Caroline Bowles, 18 December 1829

You have burnt my letters, my own Juliette, but you have not destroyed my love ... When you destroyed the letters, I know how much pain and love were in your soul. I had poured my heart into them, I had never written anything more true or more deeply felt; it was my guts, my blood, my life and thoughts during six months ... At a word of mine which you misunderstood, and which never had the unfair meaning you gave it, you destroyed everything. I have felt bitter regrets at the loss, but I have not reproached you for it. My beautiful soul, my angel, my poor darling Juliette, I understand you and love you.
VICTOR HUGO
in a letter to Juliette Drouet, October 1833

Victor, I love you. Victor, I shall die of this separation. I need you to be able to live ... I feel as though all my veins have been opened, and my life's blood has slowly been draining away. I feel as though I am dying, and I know that I love you all the more for every pang.
JULIETTE DROUET
in a letter to Victor Hugo, 5 August 1834

In love we have a thousand foolish things to say, that of themselves bear no great sound, but have a mighty sense in love; for there is a peculiar eloquence natural alone to a lover, and to be understood by no other creature.
>APHRA BEHN
>*The Lover's Watch*

Lovers, it is well known, carry the art of tautology to its utmost perfection, and even the most impatient of them can both bear to hear and repeat the same things time without number, till the sound becomes the echo to the sense or the nonsense previously uttered.
>SUSAN FERRIER
>*The Inheritance*

All the world loves a lover – unless he's in a telephone booth.
>DAVE TOMICK

Jealousy and Obsession

A really *grand passion* is comparatively rare nowadays. It is the privilege of people who have nothing to do. That is the one use of the idle classes in a country.
>OSCAR WILDE
>*A Woman of No Importance*

… a love that has taken away my reason. I can't eat. I can't sleep. I don't care for my friends. I don't care for glory. I value victory only because it pleases you … You have filled me with a limitless love … an intoxicating frenzy.
>NAPOLEON BONAPARTE
>in a letter to Josephine

I have found it impossible to carry the heavy burden of responsibility and to discharge my duties as King as I would wish to, without the help and support of the woman I love.
>EDWARD VIII
>in his abdication speech, 11 December 1936

I have been astonished that Men could die Martyrs for religion I have shudder'd at it – I shudder no more – I could be martyr'd for my Religion – Love is my religion – I could die for that – I could die for you. My Creed is Love and you are its only tenet – You have ravish'd me away by a Power I cannot resist: and yet I could resist till I saw you; and even since I have seen you I have endeavoured often 'to reason against the reasons of my Love'. I can do that no more – the pain would be too great – My Love is selfish – I cannot breathe without you. Yours for ever
>JOHN KEATS
>in a letter to Fanny Brawne, 13 October 1819

It is wicked of me to torment you, yet I cannot help myself. My offence goes by the name of 'jealousy'.
> JULIETTE DROUET
> in a letter to Victor Hugo in 1834

Jealousy, n. The seamy side of love.
> AMBROSE BIERCE
> *The Enlarged Devil's Dictionary*

Nothing is more capable of troubling our reason, and consuming our health, than secret notions of jealousy in solitude.
> APHRA BEHN
> *The History of Agnes De Castro*

You know that when I hate you, it is because I love you to a point of passion that unhinges my soul.
> JULIE DE LESPINASSE
> in a letter to the Comte de Guibert (who did not return her love) in 1774

What is so withering … is the possessiveness of love … It is a projection of that maternal or paternal cannibalism which desires to hug what belongs to it, even unto death.
> JOHN COWPER POWYS
> *The Meaning of Culture*

Love which is all-inclusive seems to repel us.
> HENRY MILLER
> *The Books in My Life*

For a time men will endure scenes of anger and jealousy from the woman they deeply love. Some prefer agitated love affairs as they prefer rough seas

to calm ones; but most of them are definitely peace-loving.
>   ANDRÉ MAUROIS
>   *The Art of Living*

I am literally worn to death, which seems my only recourse. I cannot forget what has pass'd. What? nothing with a man of the world, but to me deathful. I will get rid of this as much as possible. When you were in the habit of flirting with Brown you would have left off, could your own heart have felt one half of one pang mine did. Brown is a good sort of Man – he did not know he was doing me to death by inches. I feel the effect of every one of those hours in my side now; and for that cause, though he has done me many services, though I know his love and friendship for me, though at this moment I should be without pence were it not for his assistance, I will never see or speak to him until we are both old men, if we are to be. I *will* resent my heart having been made a football.
    JOHN KEATS
    in a letter to Fanny Brawne, *c.* May 1820

Or love me less, or love me more;
And play not with my liberty:
Either take all, or all restore;
Bind me at least, or set me free.
    SIDNEY GODOLPHIN
    'Song'

Never have I loved you more than I did yesterday, in the frenzy and jealous rage I was in … Loved you as never woman has been loved before, nor ever will be. I love you as much as to die, to kill you. Don't complain too much. There is nothing better under the sun than to be loved in this way.
    VICTOR HUGO
    in a letter to Juliette Drouet, autumn 1835

'How beautiful you are! You are more beautiful in anger than in repose. I don't ask you for your love; give me yourself and your hatred; give me yourself and that pretty rage; give me yourself and that enchanting scorn; it will be enough for me.'
CHARLES DICKENS
John Jasper declares himself to Rosa Bud, *The Mystery of Edwin Drood*

She put up her hand to clasp his neck, and bring her cheek to his as he held her; while he, in return, covering her with frantic caresses, said wildly –

'You teach me now how cruel you've been – cruel and false. *Why* did you despise me? *Why* did you betray your own heart, Cathy? I have not one word of comfort. You deserve this. You have killed yourself. Yes, you may kiss me, and cry; and wring out my kisses and tears: they'll blight you – they'll damn you. You loved me – then what *right* had you to leave me? What right – answer me – for the poor fancy you felt for Linton? Because misery, and degradation, and death, and nothing that God or satan could inflict would have parted us, *you*, of your own will, did it. I have not broken your heart – *you* have broken it; and in breaking it, you have broken mine.'
EMILY BRONTË
Wuthering Heights

'I'd rather think of you as dead than as married to another man.

'That's very selfish of you!' she returned with the ardour of a real conviction. 'If you're not happy yourself others have yet a right to be.'
HENRY JAMES
The Portrait of a Lady

Good God, hoe woman breathing can deserve halfe the trouble you give YourSelf; If I were Yours from this minute I could not recompence what you have sufferd from the Violence of your passion though I were all that you can imagin mee …

I tremble at the desperate things you say in your letter. For the Love of God consider Seriously with your selfe what can Enter into comparison with the Safety of your soule, are a thousand Women or ten thousand world's worth it?
>   DOROTHY OSBORNE
>   in a letter to William Temple, 7 January 1653/4

Is selfishness a necessary ingredient in the composition of that passion called love, or does it deserve all the fine things which poets, in the exercise of their undoubted vocation, have said of it? There are, no doubt, authenticated instances of gentlemen having given up ladies and ladies having given up gentlemen to meritorious rivals, under circumstances of great high-mindedness; but is it quite established that the majority of such ladies and gentlemen have not made a virtue of necessity, and nobly resigned what was beyond their reach?
>   CHARLES DICKENS
>   *Nicholas Nickleby*

Who promised love should be happiness? Nature may have some other end.
>   MARK RUTHERFORD
>   *Last Pages from A Journal*

Imbroglios

I became inflamed by my own style, and as I finished the letter I felt a little of the passion that I had sought to express with the greatest possible force.
    BENJAMIN CONSTANT
    Adolphe

So soon to engage in a new amour with another woman, while I fancied, and you pretended, your heart was bleeding for me? Indeed, you have acted strangely. Can I believe the passion you have profest to me to be sincere? Or, if I can, what happiness can I assure myself of with a man capable of so much inconstancy?

HENRY FIELDING
Tom Jones

'I hoped you would think all the better of me, Tina, for doing as I have done, instead of bearing malice towards me. I hoped you would see that it is the best thing for every one – the best for your happiness too.'

'Oh pray don't make love to Miss Assher for the sake of my happiness,' answered Tina.

GEORGE ELIOT
Mr Gilfil's Love-Story, Scenes of Clerical Life

Mathurine (to Don Juan): What are you doing there with Charlotte? Are you speaking to her of love as well?

Don Juan (softly to Mathurine): No. On the contrary, she is the one who expressed the wish to become my wife, and I told her I was engaged to you.

Charlotte (to Don Juan): What does Mathurine want with you?

Don Juan (softly to Charlotte): She is jealous to see me talking to you and would like me to marry her; but I told her it is you I want.

    MOLIÈRE
    Don Juan

M de Nemours' passion for Mme de Clèves was so violent at the outset that it even blotted out the memory of all the other women he had loved and with whom he had kept up relations during his absence from Court. He did not even take the trouble to find a pretext to break off with them; he did not have the patience to listen to their complaints and to answer their reproaches.

    Mme DE LA FAYETTE
    La Princesse de Clèves

Rapture

Down there we satt upon the Moss,
And did begin to play
A Thousand Amorous Tricks, to pass
The heat of all the day.
A many Kisses he did give:
And I return'd the same
Which made me willing to receive
That which I dare not name.
   APHRA BEHN
   'The Willing Mistriss'

Verbal consent should be obtained with every new level of physical and/or sexual contact or conduct in any given interaction regardless of who initiates it.
     from the sex rules manual issued at Antioch College, Ohio, October 1993

We had supper on our own; I was filled with happiness which was almost overpowering, and at the same time felt melancholy, but Henriette, who also looked sad, did not reproach me. Our sadness was in fact no more than shyness; we loved each other, but we had had no time to get to know each other. We exchanged only a few words, without saying anything witty or interesting, so that conversation seemed banal, and we found more pleasure in our own thoughts. We knew that we were going to spend the night together ... What a night! What a delightful woman was Henriette ...!
GIACOMO CASANOVA
Memoirs

O insupportable delight! O superhuman rapture! what pain could stand before a pleasure so transporting? I felt no more the smart of my wounds below; but, curling round him like the tendril of a vine, as if I fear'd any part of him should be untouch'd or unpress'd by me, I return'd his strenuous embraces and kisses with a fervour and gusto only known to true love, and which mere lust could never rise to.
    JOHN CLELAND
    Fanny Hill

'Oh Joe, I love you with all of me now, every little bit of me is yours.'
    JOHN BRAINE
    Room at the Top

But did thee feel the earth move?
    ERNEST HEMINGWAY
    For Whom the Bells Tolls

> Busie old foole, unruly Sunne,
> Why dost thou thus,
> Through windowes, and through curtaines call on us?
> Must to thy motions lovers seasons run? ...
> Love, all alike, no season knowes, nor clyme,
> Nor houres, dayes, moneths, which are the rags of time.
> JOHN DONNE
> 'The Sunne Rising'

Fortunate are lovers who, when their senses are satiated, are able to fall back on intellectual enjoyments supplied by the mind. Gentle sleep then comes to them, and lasts until the body has recovered its balance. On waking up, the senses are active again and ever ready for more play.
GIACOMO CASANOVA
Memoirs

Here began the usual tender preliminaries, as delicious, perhaps, as the crowning act of enjoyment itself; which they often beget an impatience of, that makes pleasure destructive of itself, by hurrying on the final period, and closing that scene of bliss, in which the actors are generally too well pleas'd with their parts, not to wish them an eternity of duration.
JOHN CLELAND
Fanny Hill

> Wilt thou be gone? it is not yet near day:
> It was the nightingale, and not the lark,
> That pierc'd the fearful hollow of thine ear.
> WILLIAM SHAKESPEARE
> *Romeo and Juliet*

Under the pretext of hard work, we abandoned ourselves completely to love, and those secret retreats which love needs, the study of our texts provided. And so, with our books lying open in front of us, more words of love rose to our lips than of literature, and there were more kisses than words. Our hands went to each other more often than to the pages ... What more shall I say? No stage of love was left out by us in our avidity, and if love could invent anything new, that we enjoyed as well.
>PETER ABELARD
>describing tutorials with his pupil Heloise,
>*Historia Calamitatum*

I did not have long to wait: when pleasure is the prospect, we do not dally. I fell into her arms, intoxicated with love and happiness, and for seven hours I gave her ample evidence of my ardour and my feelings for her ... Ten hours of deep sleep restored my usual vigour.
>GIACOMO CASANOVA
>*Memoirs*

A more voluptuous night I never enjoyed. Five times was I fairly lost in supreme rapture. Louisa was madly fond of me; she declared I was a prodigy, and asked me if this was not extraordinary for human nature. I said twice as much might be, but this was not, although in my own mind I was somewhat proud of my performance.
>JAMES BOSWELL
>*Journals*, 12 January 1763

Men make love more intensely at twenty, but make love better, however, at thirty.
>CATHERINE II OF RUSSIA
>in a letter

It is the fate of sensual love to become extinguished when it is satisfied; for it be able to last, it must ... be mixed with purely tender components ...
>   SIGMUND FREUD
>   *Group Psychology and the Analysis of the Ego*

I then went to Louisa and was permitted the rites of love with great complacency; yet I felt my passion for Louisa much more gone. I felt a degree of coldness for her.
>   JAMES BOSWELL
>   *Journals*, 16 January 1763

Have you not observed that pleasure, which it cannot be denied is the sole motive force behind the union of men and women, is not however sufficient to form a bond between them? And that, if it follows desire which impels, it is followed by disgust which repels?
>   CHODERLOS DE LACLOS
>   *Les Liaisons dangereuses*

Sex in a love relationship is always better. I know a lot more about sex now – there's no more of that frantic fumbling and groping that went on when you were young.
>   PAUL DANIELS

Sex is emotion in motion.
>   MAE WEST

I loved and respected Ellenore a thousand times more after she had given herself to me. I walked with pride among men; I looked around with an air of domination.
>   BENJAMIN CONSTANT
>   *Adolphe*

Females are naturally libidinous, incite the males to copulation, and cry out during the act of coition.
ARISTOTLE
Historia Animalium

How a man must hug, and dandle, and kittle, and play a hundred little tricks with his bedfellow when he is disposed to make that use of her that nature designed for her.
ERASMUS
The Praise of Folly

A man of any age can persuade himself that a woman's thighs are altar rails, and that her passion is the hosanna of virtuous love rather than the wanton tumult of nerve endings.
BEN HECHT
Gaily, Gaily

He moved his lips about her ears and neck as though in thirsting search of an erogenous zone. A waste of time, he knew from experience. Erogenous zones were either everywhere or nowhere.
JOSEPH HELLER
Good as Gold

Day by day Pericone's passion grew more ardent, being fuelled by the proximity and contrariety of its object. Seeing that blandishment got him nowhere, he decided to have recourse to wiles and stratagems, and if that failed to force. The lady, forbidden by her law to drink wine, found it, perhaps as a result, all the more to her liking; so Pericone determined to enlist Bacchus in the service of Venus, and provided one evening a supper which was laid out with all possible pomp and beauty ... He instructed the servant who waited on Alatiel to ply her with various kinds of blended wines ... She, suspecting nothing, and seduced by the delicious taste of the liquor, drank rather more freely than was seemly, and forgetting her past woes, became skittish ...

When the guests had at last gone, Pericone attended the lady alone to her chamber where, the heat of the wine overcoming the cold counsels of modesty, she made no more account of his presence than if he had been one of her women, undressed and went to bed. Pericone lost no time in following her, and as soon as the light was out lay down by her side. Taking her in his arms, without any demur on her part, he began to pleasure himself with her after the manner of lovers; which experience – she knew nothing till then of men – caused her to regret that she had not yielded to his blandishments before then; and thereafter she did not wait to be invited to such nights of delight but often declared her readiness.
    BOCCACCIO
    The Decameron

To succeed with the opposite sex, tell her you're impotent. She can't wait to disprove it.
    CARY GRANT

Thus we spent the whole afternoon till supper time, in a continued circle of love delights, kissing, turtlebilling, toying, and all the rest of the feast. At length, supper was serv'd in, before which Charles had, for I do not know what reason, slipt his clothes on; and sitting down by the bedside, we made table and table-cloth of the bed and sheets, whilst he suffer'd nobody to attend or serve but himself. He ate with a very good appetite, and seem'd charm'd to see me eat.

JOHN CLELAND
Fanny Hill

Take of love what a sober man takes of wine; do not become a drunkard.

ALFRED DE MUSSET
La Confession d'un enfant du siècle

My darling little Toto ... I am going to bed now, as I am not sure that you will come early enough to take me out; besides, you are not the sort of man to be shocked at finding a woman in bed, especially ...

JULIETTE DROUET
in a note to Victor Hugo, 4 November 1834

'Tis true, 'tis day; what though it be?
O wilt thou therefore rise from me?
Why should we rise, because 'tis light?
Did we lie downe, because 'twas night?
Love which in spight of darkness brought us
    hether,
Should in despight of light keepe us together.
   JOHN DONNE
   'Breake of Day'

Heartbreak

Falling out of love is very enlightening; for a short while you see the world with new eyes.
    IRIS MURDOCH

I cannot conceive that one might be able to lie in love ... Every time I have fallen in love with a woman, I have told her so, and every time I have stopped loving one, I have also told her so, with the same sincerity.
    ALFRED DE MUSSET
    La Confession d'un enfant du siècle

I am no longer your lover; and since you oblige me to confess it by this truly unfeminine persecution, learn that I am attached to another, whose name it would of course be dishonest to mention. I shall ever remember with gratitude the many instances I have received of the predilection you have shown in my favour. I shall ever continue your friend, if your ladyship will permit me so to style myself.

And as a proof of my regard, I offer you this advice, correct your vanity, which is ridiculous; exert your absurd caprices on others, and leave me in peace. – Your obedient servant,
    LORD BYRON
    in a letter to Lady Caroline Lamb, 1812

Lady Caroline stabbed herself at Lady Ilchester's ball for the love of Lord Byron. What a charming thing to be a Poet ... I never heard of a Lady doing herself the smallest mischief on my account.
    REVD SYDNEY SMITH
    in a letter in 1813

You do not love me any more, you do not love me any more – that much is clear. I was feeling really ill when you left last night. You could see that I was, but you still left. You were right to do so; you were tired. But today, I haven't had word from you. You did not even send round to find out how I was. I was hoping you would come, and waited every minute from eleven o'clock in the morning to midnight. What a day! Every time the bell went I jumped out of my skin. As a result I feel physically ill. Oh if only I could die! You still love me with your senses, and I too love you in this way better than ever … But I also love you with all my soul, while you don't even feel friendship for me … How sad, it really is finished.
> GEORGE SAND
> suffering in the final weeks of her affair with
> Alfred de Musset, November 1834
> *Journal Intime*

I went back to my room; indifferent to the future, weighed down by the most violent grief, I locked myself in, and went to bed. I felt so depressed that I was prostrate. Life was not a burden only in that I did not give it a thought. I was in a state of complete moral and physical apathy.
> GIACOMO CASANOVA
> after parting with one of his mistresses
> *Memoirs*

We are never so defenceless against suffering as when we love, never so forlornly unhappy as when we have lost our love-object or its love.
> SIGMUND FREUD
> *Civilization and Its Discontents*

Marianne would have thought herself very inexcusable had she been able to sleep at all the first night after parting from Willoughby. She would have been ashamed to look her family in the face the next morning, had she not risen from her bed in more need of repose than when she lay down in it. But the feelings which made such composure a disgrace, left her in no danger of incurring it. She was awake the whole night, and she wept the greatest part of it. She got up with an headache, was unable to talk, and unwilling to take any nourishment; giving pain every moment to her mother and sister, and forbidding all attempt at consolation from either.
    JANE AUSTEN
    Sense and Sensibility

Passion in a dromedary doesn't go so deep;
A camel when it's mating never sobs itself to sleep.
    NOEL COWARD

To make her love him so – to speak such tender words – to give her such caresses, and then to behave as if such things had never been. He had given her the poison that seemed so sweet when she was drinking it, and now it was in her blood, and she was helpless.

With this tempest pent up in her bosom, the poor child went up to her room every night, and there it all burst forth. There with loud whispers and sobs, restlessly pacing up and down, lying on the hard floor, courting cold and weariness, she told to the pitiful listening night the anguish which she could pour into no mortal ear.
    GEORGE ELIOT
    Mr Gilfil's Love-Story, Scenes of Clerical Life

Love and Misery proverbially go together. There is a popular notion ... that a lover could not get along without a little misery.
FRANCES GREVILLE

Hell's afloat in lovers' tears.
DOROTHY PARKER

> Had we never lov'd sae kindly,
> Had we never lov'd sae blindly,
> Never met – or never parted,
> We had ne'er been broken hearted.
>> ROBERT BURNS
>> 'Ae Fond Kiss'

The beginning and the decline of love are both marked by the embarrassment the lovers feel to be alone together.
> LA BRUYERE
> *Les Caractères*

> We were two lovers standing sadly by
> While our two loves lay dead upon the ground;
> Each love had striven not to be first to die,
> But each was gashed with many a cruel wound.
> Said I: 'Your love was false while mine was true.'
> Aflood with tears he cried: 'It was not so,
> 'Twas your false love my true love falsely slew –
> For 'twas your love that was the first to go.'
>> SAMUEL BUTLER
>> *Note-Books*

Love is sweet in the beginning but sour in the ending.
> OLD ENGLISH PROVERB

It is a terrible thing not to be loved when one loves; but it is also terrible to be loved with passion when one no longer loves.
> BENJAMIN CONSTANT
> *Adolphe*

The fickleness of the women whom I love is only equalled by the infernal constancy of the women who love me.
> BERNARD SHAW

Only time can heal your broken heart, just as only time can heal his broken arms and legs.
 MISS PIGGY
 Miss Piggy's Guide to Life, 1981

Don't think that every sad-eyed woman has loved and lost – she may have got him.
 ANON

Time does not bring relief; you all have lied
Who told me time would ease me of my pain!
I miss him in the weeping of the rain;
I want him at the shrinking of the tide …
    EDNA ST VINCENT MILLAY
    'Sonnet'

To the greatest joys have succeeded the greatest sorrows.
    HELOISE
    in a letter to Abelard

Give me back the lost delight
That once my soul possessed,
When love was loveliest.
    LOUISE MOLTON
    'Tonight'

She was still too intoxicated with that momentary revival of old emotions, too much agitated by the sudden return of tenderness in her lover, to know whether pain or pleasure predominated. It was as if a miracle had happened in her little world of feeling, and made the future all vague – a dim morning haze of possibilities, instead of the sombre wintry daylight and clear rigid outline of painful certainty.
    GEORGE ELIOT
    Mr Gilfil's Love-Story, Scenes of Clerical Life

Of Marriage

There is no greater risk, perhaps, than matrimony, but there is nothing happier than a happy marriage.
>   BENJAMIN DISRAELI
>   in a letter to Princess Louise, on her
>   engagement to the Marquess of Lorne, in 1870

Marriage enlarges the scene of our happiness and miseries. A marriage of love is pleasant; a marriage of interest easy; and a marriage where both meet, happy.
>   JOSEPH ADDISON
>   *The Spectator*

'Tis a hazard both ways I confess, to live single or to marry ... It may be bad, it may be good, as it is a cross and calamity on the one side, so 'tis a sweet delight, an incomparable happiness, a blessed estate, a most unspeakable benefit, a sole content, on the other, 'tis all in the proof. Be not then so wayward, so covetous, so distrustful, so curious and nice, but let's all marry.
    ROBERT BURTON
    The Anatomy of Melancholy

Holy and intimate is this union of man and wife as no other can be, and you can never give your parents more happiness and comfort than when they know and see that you are a truly devoted, loving and useful wife to your dear husband.
    QUEEN VICTORIA
    in a letter to Princess Vicky, 25 January 1858

Boswell: 'Pray, Sir, do you not suppose that there are fifty women in the world, with any one of whom a man may be as happy, as with any one woman in particular?' *Johnson*: 'Ay, Sir, fifty thousand.' *Boswell*: 'Then, Sir, you are not of opinion with some who imagine that certain men and certain women are made for each other; and that they cannot be happy if they miss their counterparts?' *Johnson*: 'To be sure not, Sir. I believe marriages would in general be as happy, and often more so, if they were all made by the Lord Chancellor, upon a due consideration of characters and circumstances, without the parties having any choice in the matter.'
    JAMES BOSWELL
    Life of Johnson

People often say that marriage is an important thing, and should be much thought of in advance, and marrying people are cautioned that there are many who marry in haste and repent at leisure. I am not sure, however, that marriage may not be pondered over too much; nor do I feel certain that the leisurely repentance does not as often follow the leisurely marriages as it does the rapid ones. That some repent no one can doubt; but I am inclined to believe that most men and women take their lots as they find them, marrying as the birds do by force of nature, and going on with their mates with a general, though not perhaps an undisturbed satisfaction, feeling inwardly assured that Providence, if it have not done the very best for them, has done for them as well as they could do for themselves with all the thought in the world. I do not know that a woman can assure to herself, by her own prudence and taste, a good husband any more than she can add two cubits to her stature; but husbands have been made to be decently good, – and wives too, for the most part, in our country, – so that the thing does not require quite so much thinking as some people say.
    ANTHONY TROLLOPE
    Can You Forgive Her?

Men and women, in marrying, make a vow to love one another. Would it not be better for their happiness if they made a vow to please one another?
    STANISLAUS LESZCYNSKI, king of Poland
    Oeuvres du philosophe bienfaisant, 1763

There are good marriages, but none that are delightful.
    LA ROCHEFOUCAULD
    Maximes

If marriages are made in Heaven, they should be happier.
>   THOMAS SOUTHERNE
>   *Isabella*, or *The Fatal Marriage*

What an Age doe wee live in where 'tis a Miracle if in ten Couple that are marryed two of them live soe as not to publish it to the world that they cannot agree …

'Tis a sad thing when all on's happinesse is only that ye world dos not know you are miserable, for my part I think it were very convenient that all such as intend to marrye should live together in the same house some year's of probation and if in all that time they never disagreed they should then bee permitted to marry if they pleased. But how few would doe it then!
>   DOROTHY OSBORNE
>   in a letter to William Temple, October 1653

Inoculation, or a hair of the dog that is going to bite you – this principle should be introduced in respect of marriage and speculation.
>   SAMUEL BUTLER
>   *Note-Books*

One should always be in love. That is the reason one should never marry.
>   OSCAR WILDE
>   *A Woman of No Importance*

A great many people fall in love with or feel attracted to a person who offers the least possibility of a harmonious union.
>   DR RUDOLF DREIKURS
>   *The Challenge of Marriage*

Love as a relation between men and women was ruined by the desire to make sure of the legitimacy of children.
>   BERTRAND RUSSELL
>   *Marriage and Morals*

I don't think marriage is the romantic idyll. It is not about the never, never land, it is a contract drawn up between two people based on love but also on certain values and certain concerns.
>   RABBI JULIA NEUBERGER
>   speaking at a debate in April 1993

What has changed is not marital happiness but expectation of it. Our generation is much more likely to complain, 'The romance has gone out of our relationship', and seek a remedy for such dissatisfaction.
>   CLAIRE RAYNER
>   writing in the *Sunday Times*, December 1993

For a marriage to last it must be one long affair.
>   ANON

I mentioned a friend of mine having resolved never to marry a pretty woman. *Johnson*: 'Sir, it is a very foolish resolution to resolve not to marry a pretty woman. Beauty is of itself very estimable. No, Sir, I would prefer a pretty woman, unless there are objections to her. A pretty woman may be foolish; a pretty woman may be wicked; a pretty woman may not like me. But there is no such danger in marrying a pretty woman as is apprehended ... A pretty woman, if she has a mind to be wicked, can find a readier way than another, and that is all.'
SAMUEL JOHNSON
Boswell's *Life of Johnson*

Many a man in love with a dimple makes the mistake of marrying the wrong girl.
STEPHEN LEACOCK
Literary Lapses

The great use of female beauty, the great practical advantage of it is, that it naturally and unavoidably tends to keep the husband in good humour with himself, to make him, to use the dealer's phrase, pleased with his bargain. When old age approaches, and the parties have become endeared to each other by a long series of joint cares and interests, and when children have come and bound them together by the strongest ties that nature has in store, at this age the features and the person are of less consequence; but in the young days of matrimony, when the roving eye of the bachelor is scarcely become steady in the head of the husband, it is dangerous for him to see, every time he stirs out, a face more captivating than that of the person to whom he is bound for life.
WILLIAM COBBETT
Advice to Young Men and (Incidentally) to Young Women, 1829

It isn't tying himself to one woman that a man dreads when he thinks of marrying; it's separating himself from all the others.

    HELEN ROWLAND

One (woman) is pretty nearly as good as another, as far as any judgement can be formed of them before marriage. It is only after marriage that they show their true qualities, as I know by bitter experience. Marriage is, therefore, a lottery.

    THOMAS LOVE PEACOCK
    Nightmare Abbey

I hope, my dear Ellison, you will do me the justice to believe me when I assure you that the love I have for you is founded on the sacred principles of virtue and honour, and by consequence so long as you continue possessed of those amiable qualities which first inspired my passion for you, so long must I continue to love you.

Believe me, my dear, it is love like this alone which can render the marriage state happy. People may talk of flames and raptures as long as they please – and a warm fancy with a flow of youthful spirits may make them feel something like what they describe; but sure I am the nobler faculties of the mind, with kindred feelings of the heart, can only be the foundation of friendship, and it has always been my opinion that the married life was only friendship in a more exalted degree.

    ROBERT BURNS
    in a letter to Ellison Begbie

Proposals

There are a great many ways of proposing. All of them are good. In fact, experience teaches that unless you are very careless in the way you propose, you are in positive danger of being accepted.
    FRANK RICHARDSON
    Love and All About It

Even at that moment he was in doubt. But he would write his letter to Miss Dunstable and see how it looked. He was almost determined not to send it; so, at least, he said to himself: but he could do no harm by writing it. So he did write it, as follows: – 'Greshamsbury, June, 185-. My dear Miss Dunstable –' When he had got so far, he leaned back in his chair and looked at the paper. How on earth was he to find words to say that which he now wished to have said? He had never written such a letter in his life.
    ANTHONY TROLLOPE
    Dr Thorne proposes, *Framley Parsonage*

I don't know how I did it. I did it in a moment. I intercepted Jip. I had Dora in my arms. I was full of eloquence. I never stopped for a word. I told her how I loved her. I told her I should die without her. I told her that I idolised and worshipped her. Jip barked madly all the time.

When Dora hung her head and cried, and trembled, my eloquence increased so much the more. If she would like me to die for her, she had but to say the word, and I was ready. Life without Dora's love was not a thing to have on any terms. I couldn't bear it, and I wouldn't. I had loved her every minute, every day and night, since I first saw her. I loved her at that minute to distraction. I should always love her, every minute, to distraction. Lovers had loved before, and lovers would love again; but no lover had ever loved, might, could, would, or should ever love, as I loved Dora.

CHARLES DICKENS
David Copperfield

'Ah!' he said, slowly turning his eyes towards me. 'Well! if you was writin' to her, p'raps you'd recollect to say that Barkis was willin'; would you?'

'That Barkis is willing,' I repeated, innocently. 'Is that all the message?'

'Yes-es,' he said, considering. 'Ye-es. Barkis is willin'.'

CHARLES DICKENS
David Copperfield

After that, love, bliss and rapture; rapture, love and bliss. Be mine, be mine!'

CHARLES DICKENS
Mrs Nickleby receives a proposal
Nicholas Nickleby

Algernon missed a splendid race. Let us hope he won Lucy. From *Punch* in 1875.

Jack: Gwendolen, will you marry me? (*Goes on his knees.*)
Gwendolen: Of course I will, darling. How long you have been about it! I am afraid you have had very little experience in how to propose.
    OSCAR WILDE
    The Importance of Being Earnest

'My present salary, Miss Summerson, at Kenge and Carboy's, is two pound a week. When I first had the happiness of looking upon you, it was one-fifteen, and had stood at that figure for a lengthened period. A rise of five has since taken place, and a further rise of five is guaranteed at the expiration of a term not exceeding twelve months from the present date. My mother has a little property, which takes the form of a small life annuity; upon which she lives in an independent though unassuming manner, in the Old Street Road. She is eminently calculated for a mother-in-law. She never interferes, is all for peace, and her disposition easy. She has her failings – as who has not? – but I never knew her to do it when company was present; at which time you may freely trust her with wines, spirits, or malt liquors. My own abode is lodgings at Penton Place, Pentonville. It is lowly, but airy, open at the back, and considered one of the 'ealthiest outlets. Miss Summerson! In the mildest language, I adore you. Would you be so kind as to allow me (as I may say) to file a declaration – to make an offer!'
    CHARLES DICKENS
    Mr Guppy proposes, *Bleak House*

Maldives this year. Holiday as Puss or honeymoon as Mrs Bear?
    Valentine message in *The Times*, February 1994

'Are you – are you very poor?'

'I am but a wanderer,' said Walter, 'making voyages to live across the sea. That is my calling now.'

'Are you soon going away again, Walter?'

'Very soon.'

She sat looking at him for a moment; then timidly put her trembling hand in his.

'If you will take me for your wife, Walter, I will love you dearly. If you will let me go with you, Walter, I will go to the world's end without fear. I can give up nothing for you – I have nothing to resign, and no one to forsake; but all my love and life shall be devoted to you, and with my last breath I will breathe your name to God if I have sense and memory left.'

He caught her to his heart, and laid her cheek against his own, and now, no more repulsed, no more forlorn, she wept indeed, upon the breast of her dear lover.

CHARLES DICKENS
Florence Dombey finds love, *Dombey and Son*

'At what particular point did you mention the word marriage, Dorian? And what did she say in answer? Perhaps you forgot all about it.'

'My dear Harry, I did not treat it as a business transaction, and I did not make any formal proposal. I told her that I loved her, and she said she was not worthy to be my wife. Not worthy! Why, the whole world is nothing to me compared with her.'

'Women are wonderfully practical,' murmured Lord Henry – 'much more practical than we are. In situations of that kind we often forget to say anything about marriage, and they always remind us.'

OSCAR WILDE
The Picture of Dorian Gray

At about ½ p. 12 I sent for Albert; he came to the Closet where I was alone, and after a few minutes I said to him, that I thought he must be aware why I wished (him) to come here, and that it would make me too happy if he would consent to what I wished; we embraced each other over and over again, and he was so kind, so affectionate. Oh! to feel I was, and am, loved by such an Angel as Albert was too great delight to describe! he is perfection; perfection in every way – in beauty – in everything! I told him I was quite unworthy of him and kissed his dear hand – he said he would be very happy [to share his life with her] and was so kind and seemed so happy, that I really felt it was the happiest brightest moment in my life.

    QUEEN VICTORIA
    Journal, 15 October 1839

Oh Bernard she sighed fervently I certinly love you madly you are to me like a Heathen god she cried looking at his manly form and handsome flashing face I will indeed marry you.
    DAISY ASHORD
    The Young Visiters

'What is the matter? you are distressed. Tell me – pray.'

Rosamond had never been spoken to in such tones before. I am not sure that she knew what the words were; but she looked at Lydgate and the tears fell over her cheeks. There could have been no more complete answer than that silence, and Lydgate, forgetting everything else, completely mastered by the outrush of tenderness at the sudden belief that this sweet young creature depended on him for her joy, actually put his arms round her, folding her gently and protectingly – he was used to being gentle with the weak and suffering – and kissed each of the two large tears. This was a strange way of arriving at an understanding, but it was a short way. Rosamond was not angry, but she moved backward a little in timid happiness, and Lydgate could now sit near her and speak less incompletely. Rosamond had to make her little confession, and he poured out words of gratitude and tenderness with impulsive lavishment. In half an hour he left the house an engaged man, whose soul was not his own, but the woman's to whom he had bound himself.

    GEORGE ELIOT
    Middlemarch

'Oh, my Lord,' exclaimed I, 'rise, I beseech you, rise! – such a posture to me! – surely your Lordship is not so cruel as to mock me!'

'Mock you!' repeated he earnestly; 'no, I revere you! I esteem and I admire you above all human beings! You are the friend to whom my soul is

attached as to its better half! You are the most amiable, the most perfect of women! and you are dearer to me than language has the power of telling.'

I attempt not to describe my sensations at that moment; I scarce breathed; I doubted if I existed, – the blood forsook my cheeks, and my feet refused to sustain me: Lord Orville, hastily rising, supported me to a chair, upon which I sunk, almost lifeless.

    FANNY BURNEY
    Evelina

'You are too generous to trifle with me. If your feelings are still what they were last April, tell me so at once. *My* affections and wishes are unchanged; but one word from you will silence me on this subject for ever.'

Elizabeth, feeling all the more than common awkwardness and anxiety of his situation, now forced herself to speak; and immediately, though not very fluently, gave him to understand that her sentiments had undergone so material a change since the period to which he alluded, as to make her receive with gratitude and pleasure his present assurances. The happiness which this reply produced was such as he had probably never felt before, and he expressed himself on the occasion as sensibly and as warmly as a man violently in love can be supposed to do.

    JANE AUSTEN
    Pride and Prejudice

'Oh, Flora, let us be man and wife. You at least understand me – the only woman who ever did!'

'Oh yes, I understand you well enough, Algernon. But how about your ever being able to understand *me*?'

    old PUNCH cartoon, September 1896

Gabriel looked her long in the face, but the firelight being faint there was not much to be seen.

'Bathsheba,' he said, tenderly and in surprise, and coming closer: 'If I only knew one thing – whether you would allow me to love you and win you, and marry you after all – if I only knew that!'

'But you never will know,' she murmured.

'Why?'

'Because you never ask.'
>   THOMAS HARDY
>   *Far from the Madding Crowd*

Sophie Andreyevna, I cannot go on in this way. For the last three weeks I have been saying to myself: 'I shall tell her today', and yet I keep on going away feeling the same mixture of sadness, regret, fear as well as happiness in my heart. Every night I go over the day and curse myself for not having spoken to you, and wonder what words I would have used if I *had* spoken. I am taking this letter with me, so that I can hand it to you if my courage fails me yet again.
>   LEO TOLSTOY
>   in a letter to his future wife, September 1862

'It's almost enough to make us get married after all, isn't it?' said Tim.

'Oh nonsense!' replied Miss La Creevy, laughing. 'We are too old.'

'Not a bit,' said Tim, 'we are too old to be single. Why shouldn't we both be married, instead of sitting through the long winter evenings by our solitary firesides? Why shouldn't we make one fireside of it, and marry each other?' ... Let's be a comfortable couple, and take care of each other! And if we should get deaf, or lame, or blind, or bed-ridden, how glad we shall be that we have somebody we are fond of, always to talk to and sit with! Let's be a comfortable couple. Now, do, my dear!'

Five minutes after this honest and straight-forward speech, little Miss La Creevy and Tim were talking as pleasantly as if they had been married for a score of years, and had never once quarrelled all the time.
    CHARLES DICKENS
    Nicholas Nickleby

King Henry: ... I'faith, Kate, my wooing is fit for thy understanding: I am glad thou canst speak no better English; for, if thou couldst, thou wouldst find me such a plain king that thou wouldst think I had sold my farm to buy my crown. I know no ways to mince it in love, but directly to say 'I love you': then if you urge me farther than to say 'Do you in faith?' I wear out my suit. Give your answer; i'faith, do: and so clap hands and a bargain: how say you, lady?
    WILLIAM SHAKESPEARE
    Henry V

I shall affect plainness and sincerity in my discourse to you, as much as other lovers do perplexity and rapture. Instead of saying, 'I shall die for you', I profess I should be glad to lead my life with you. You are as beautiful, as witty, as prudent, and as good-humoured as any woman breathing; but I must confess to you, I regard all these excellences as you will be pleased to direct them for my happiness or misery.

With me, madam, the only lasting motive to love is the hope of its becoming mature.

>RICHARD STEELE
>in a letter to Mary Scurlock, 11 August 1707

You know my unhappy temper. You know all my faults. It is painful to repeat them. Will you, then, knowing me fully, accept of me for your husband as I now am – not the heir of Auchinleck, but one who has had his time of the world, and is henceforth to expect no more than £100 a year? With that and the interest of your £1,000, we can live in an agreeable retirement in any part of Europe that you please. But we are to bid adieu for ever to this country. All our happiness is to be our society with each other, and our hopes of a better world. I confess this scheme is so romantic that nothing but such love as you showed at Donaghadee could make you listen to it ... Upon my honour, I would not propose it now, were I not fully persuaded that I would share a kingdom with you if I had it.

>JAMES BOSWELL
>in a letter to Margaret Montgomerie, 20 July 1769

J.B. with £100 a year is every bit as valuable to me as if possessed of the estate of Auchinleck.

>MARGARET MONTGOMERIE
>in her answer to Boswell's proposal

In his Utopia [Sir Thomas More's] his lawe is that the young people are to see each other stark naked before marriage.

Sir William Roper, of Eltham, in Kent, came one morning pretty early, to my lord, with a proposall to marry one of his daughters. My lord's daughters were then both together abed in a truckle-bed in their father's chamber asleep. He carries Sir William into the chamber and takes the sheete by the corner and suddenly whippes it off. They lay on their backs and their Smocks up as high as their armpitts. This awakened them, and immediately they turned on their Bellies. Quoth Roper, 'I have seen both sides,' and so gave a patt on her Buttock, he made choice (of Margaret) sayeing, 'Thou art mine.'
    JOHN AUBREY
    Brief Lives, 1693

She never had a proposal, only propositions.
    ALEXANDER KING
    Mine Enemy Grows Older

Dear Miss Scurlock, I am tired with calling you by that name; therefore, say the day in which you will take that of, Madam, Your most obedient, most devoted, humble servant.
    RICHARD STEELE
    in a letter to Mary Scurlock, August 1707

Rejection

'Adorable Elizabeth! Most heavenly –'

He climbed on to the sofa beside her and tried to kiss her cheek.

'Please, Mr Temple.' Then she broke into sheer disgust. 'Oh, go away! No, I do not love you. I can never love you. I do not even care for you. No, not even with friendly feelings. This is absurd. This is too absurd –'

She freed herself and stood with her hand on the bell-rope.

He was amazed. He could not believe his ears. This was the first proposal of his life, for he had always believed that himself and his riches were irresistible and that when the time did come for him to honour anybody there could be but one possible result.

HUGH WALPOLE
The Herries Chronicle

'You can't possibly go away feeling like that,' And she stared up at him frowning, biting her lip.

'Oh, that's all right,' said Reggie, giving himself a shake. 'I'll … I'll –' And he waved his hand as much as to say 'get over it.'

'But this is awful,' said Anne. She clasped her hands and stood in front of him. 'Surely you do see how fatal it would be for us to marry, don't you?'

'Oh, quite, quite,' said Reggie, looking at her with haggard eyes …

'Then why, if you understand, are you so un-unhappy?' she wailed. 'Why do you mind so fearfully? Why do you look so aw-awful?'

> KATHERINE MANSFIELD
> *Mr and Mrs Dove*

My nature demands that my life shall be perpetual love … You have struck deep. You have done that which my enemies have yet failed to do: you have broken my spirit. From the highest to the humblest scene of my life, from the brilliant world of fame to my own domestic hearth, you have poisoned all. I have no place of refuge: home is odious, the world oppressive.

> BENJAMIN DISRAELI
> in a letter to Mary Anne Wyndham Lewis, 7 February 1839. They in fact married later that year.

I will not attempt to describe what I felt on receiving your letter. I read it over and over again and again, and though it was in the politest language of refusal still it was peremptory, 'you were sorry you could not make me a return, but you wish me' – what, without you, I never can obtain – 'you wish me all kind of happiness.' It would be weak and unmanly to say that without you I never can be happy; but sure I am that sharing life with you would have given it a relish,

that, wanting you, I can never taste.... I had formed the most delightful images and my fancy fondly brooded over them: but now I am wretched for the loss of what I really had no right to expect. I must now think no more of you as a mistress, still I presume to ask to be admitted as a friend.
ROBERT BURNS
on being turned down by Ellison Begbie

... something less snappy and a good deal more glutinous was obviously indicated.
P.G. WODEHOUSE
Right ho, Jeeves
Bertie acts as intermediary between Gussie Fink-Nottle and Madeleine Bassett

We Are Engaged

An engaged woman is always more agreeable than a disengaged. She is satisfied with herself. Her cares are over, and she feels that she may exert all her powers of pleasing without suspicion. All is safe with a lady engaged; no harm can be done.
    JANE AUSTEN
    Mansfield Park

When any two young people take it into their heads to marry, they are pretty sure by perseverance to carry their point, be they ever so poor, or ever so imprudent, or ever so little likely to be necessary to each other's ultimate comfort.
    JANE AUSTEN
    Persuasion

'We are not going to be married yet. Because everything is to be got ready. And I don't want to be married so very soon, because I think it is nice to be engaged. And we shall be married all our lives after.'
    GEORGE ELIOT
    Middlemarch

Millamant: ... I won't be called names after I'm married; positively I won't be called names.
Mirabell: Names!
Millamant: Ay, as wife, spouse, my dear, joy, jewel, love, sweetheart, and the rest of that nauseous cant, in which men and their wives are so fulsomely familiar – I shall never bear that – good Mirabell, don't let us be familiar or fond, nor kiss before folks ...
>WILLIAM CONGREVE
>Millamant lays down her conditions for marriage, *The Way of the World*

I am by no means pleased with all this writing. I have told you how much I dislike it, and yet you still persist in asking me to write, and that by return of post.

O! you are really quite out of your senses. I should not have indulged you in that whim of yours, had you not given me that hint that my silence gives an air of mystery....

Before I conclude this famous epistle, I will give you a little hint – that is, not to put so many *must* in your letters – it is beginning *rather too soon*; and another thing is, that I take the liberty not to mind them much, but I expect you mind me.

You *must* take care of yourself, you *must* think of me and believe me yours sincerely,
>CHARLOTTE CARPENTER
>in a letter to Sir Walter Scott, 25 October 1797, shortly after their engagement

'We have been rash, I fear; and have done what we have done without sufficient thought.'

'I don't say that at all.'

'But I do. It does seem now that we have been imprudent.' Then she smiled as she completed her speech. 'There had better be no engagement between us.'

'Why do you say that?'

'Because it is quite clear that it has been a trouble to you rather than a happiness.'

'I wouldn't give it up for all the world.'

'But it will be better. I had not thought about it as I should have done. I did not understand that the prospect of marrying would make you – so very poor. I see it now.'

ANTHONY TROLLOPE
Adelaide Palliser offers to end the engagement, *Phineas Redux*

Cecily: It would hardly have been a really serious engagement if it hadn't been broken off at least once. But I forgave you before the week was out.

OSCAR WILDE
The Importance of Being Earnest

'Can it be that it is all over?' she thought. 'Can it be that all this has happened so quickly and has destroyed all that went before?' She recalled her love for Prince Andrew in all its former strength, and at the same time felt that she loved Kuragin. She vividly pictured herself as Prince Andrew's wife, and the scenes of happiness with him she had so often repeated in her imagination, and at the same time, aglow with excitement, recalled every detail of yesterday's interview with Anatole.

LEO TOLSTOY
War and Peace

'Mercy – shall we elope?' she laughed.
'If you would –'
'You *do* love me, Newland! I'm so happy.'
'But then – why not be happier?'
'We can't behave like people in novels, though, can we?'

EDITH WHARTON
The Age of Innocence

If it were not for the presents, an elopement would be preferable.

GEORGE ADE
Forty Modern Fables, 1901

I tremble for what we are doing. Are you sure you will love me for ever? Shall we never repent? I fear and I hope.

I foresee all that will happen on this occasion. I shall incense my family in the highest degree. The generality of the world will blame my conduct, and

An Elopement Foiled

the relations and friends of —— [the man her father wished her to marry] will invent a thousand stories of me. Yet, 'tis possible you may recompense everything to me.
>   LADY MARY WORTLEY MONTAGU
>   in a letter to Edward Wortley Montagu, 15 August 1712, just before their elopement

Oh, my dearest Friend! be always *so* good to me, and I shall make the best and happiest wife. When I read in your looks and words that you love me, I feel it in the deepest part of my soul; then I care not one straw for the whole Universe beside; but when you fly from my caresses to – smoke tobacco, or speak of me as a new *circumstance* of your lot, then indeed, my 'heart is troubled about many things' …
>   JANE WELSH CARLYLE
>   in a letter to Thomas Carlyle, 3 October 1826, shortly before their wedding

Romance is the icing but love is the cake.
>   ANON

During our three-week engagement, Renaud was always round. I loved him to distraction …, and I would have been all his as soon as he wanted, as he very well knew. And yet, like a gourmet holding back from his enjoyment, he kept us in exhausting chastity.
>   WILLY and COLETTE
>   *Claudine en Ménage*

My last blessing as a Lover is with you; this is my last letter to Jane Welsh; my first blessing as a Husband, my first kiss to Jane Carlyle is at hand! O my Darling! I will always love thee.

Good-night, then, for the last time we have to part! In a week I see you, in a week you are my own!
>THOMAS CARLYLE
>in a letter to Jane Welsh, 9 October 1826, just before their wedding

Wedding Bells

Altar: The forge where hearts are fused. From the word *halter*, to hitch.
   OLIVER HERFORD
   Cupid's Cyclopedia, 1910

When two people are under the influence of the most violent, most insane, most delusive, and most transient of passions, they are required to swear that they will remain in that excited, abnormal, and exhausting condition continuously until death do them part.
   BERNARD SHAW
   Preface to *Getting Married*

The Wedding March always reminds me of the music played when soldiers go into battle.
   HEINRICH HEINE

I wore a white satin gown with a very deep flounce of Honiton lace, imitation of old. I wore my Turkish diamond necklace and earrings, and Albert's beautiful sapphire brooch ... The Ceremony was very imposing, and fine and simple, and I think ought to make an everlasting impression on every one who promises at the Altar to keep what he or she promises. Dearest Albert repeated everything very distinctly. I felt so happy when the ring was put on, and by Albert.
   QUEEN VICTORIA
   Journal, 10 February 1840

I always pity the bridegroom on these occasions. The bride is supported by her father, and attended by her bridesmaids, and everybody is or pretends to be in a fright, lest she should faint or cry; and she has all the protection of a veil in case she should be too shy, or not shy enough; and there is a general sympathy in her feelings. The poor man has to walk himself up alone to the altar, where he stands, looking uncommonly foolish. There is the mother sobbing at him for carrying off her child; the sisters scowling at him because he did not choose one of them; the clergyman frowning at him for not producing the ring at the right moment, or for neglecting the responses in their proper places; the brothers laugh at him; the bride turns from him; and the only person who pays him the slightest attention is the clerk, who tells him when he is to kneel, and when to stand, and which is his right hand, and which his left, and helps him to the discovery of his waistcoat pocket, in which the ring may or may not be.

    EMILY EDEN
    The Semi-Attached Couple

'My God,' he thought, '*have* I got the ring?' – and once more he went through the bridegroom's convulsive gesture.

Then, in a moment, May was beside him, such radiance streaming from her that it sent a faint warmth through his numbness, and he straightened himself and smiled into her eyes.

'Dearly beloved, we are gathered together here,' the Rector began …

The ring was on her hand, the Bishop's benediction had been given, the bridesmaids were a-poise to resume their place in the procession, and the organ was showing preliminary symptoms of breaking out into the Mendelssohn March, without which no newly-wedded couple had ever emerged upon New York.

    EDITH WHARTON
    The Age of Innocence

The wedding was very much like other weddings, where the parties have no taste for finery or parade; and Mrs Elton, from the particulars detailed by her husband, thought it all extremely shabby, and very inferior to her own. 'Very little white satin, very few lace veils; a most pitiful business! …'

    JANE AUSTEN
    Emma

Clergyman: 'Wilt thou have this woman to thy wedded wife?'
Bridegroom: Well, I was told it would have to be her. But I would rather have her sister.' From *Punch* in 1878.

Reader, I married him. A quiet wedding we had: he and I, the parson and clerk, were alone present. When we got back from church, I went into the kitchen of the manor-house, where Mary was cooking the dinner, and John cleaning the knives, and I said –

'Mary, I have been married to Mr Rochester this morning.' ... Mary, bending again over the roast, said only –

'Have you, miss? Well, for sure!'
    CHARLOTTE BRONTË
    Jane Eyre

There was a little dancing, no excessive gaiety, but every face shone with real satisfaction. The weather

was lovely. Even the sun, which had hidden his face for many days, shed his warm beams upon us as we drove to church, as if to bless our union. It was a day without a jar, and I may thus enter it in this book as the fairest and most momentous of my life.
>CLARA WIECK
>diary entry describing her wedding to Robert Schumann, 12 September 1840

They all gave place when the signing was done, and Little Dorrit and her husband walked out of the church alone. They paused for a moment on the steps of the portico, looking at the fresh perspective of the street in the autumn morning's sun's bright rays, and then went down.
>CHARLES DICKENS
>*Little Dorrit*

In June she married Tom Buchanan of Chicago, with more pomp and circumstance than Louisville ever knew before. He came down with a hundred people in four private cars, and hired a whole floor of the Muhlbach Hotel, and the day before the wedding he gave her a string of pearls valued at three hundred and fifty thousand dollars.
>F. SCOTT FITZGERALD
>*The Great Gatsby*

I'm determined this will be the best wedding I have ever had.
>ELIZABETH TAYLOR
>after spending £1 million on her ninth wedding

Nearly all the couples I have married have had children present at the ceremony, but I never worry about things like this.
>REVD RON LEATHERBARROW
>vicar of St Mark's, Manchester, reported in *The Times*, October 1993

'Therefore,' says Cousin Feenix, 'I congratulate the family of which I am a member, on the acquisition of my friend Dombey. I congratulate my friend Dombey on his union with my lovely and accomplished relative who possesses every requisite to make a man happy; and I take the liberty of calling on you all, in point of fact, to congratulate both my friend Dombey and my lovely and accomplished relative, on the present occasion.'
>CHARLES DICKENS
>Cousin Feenix proposes a toast at Mr Dombey's wedding to Edith, *Dombey and Son*

Among the rest of the company there was got in a fellow you call a 'wag'. This ingenious person is the usual life of all feasts and merriments, by speaking absurdities, and putting everybody of breeding and modesty out of countenance. As soon as we sat down he drank to the bride's diversion that night; and then made twenty double meanings on the word 'thing'.
>RICHARD STEELE
>writing as Mr Bickerstaff, *The Tatler*, 1709/11

One year of joy, another of comfort, and all the rest of content.
>JOHN RAY
>proverbial marriage wish

In all the wedding cake, hope is the sweetest of the plums.
>DOUGLAS JERROLD

I always say a girl must get married for love – and keep on getting married until she finds it.
>ZSA ZSA GABOR

The Honeymoon

Blessings, in abundance come,
To the Bride, and to her Groome;
May the Bed, and this short night,
Know the fullness of delight!
Pleasures many, here attend ye
And ere long, a Boy, love send ye
Curld and comely, and so trimme,
Maides (in time) may ravish him.
    ROBERT HERRICK

When day dawned (for we did not sleep much) and I beheld that beautiful angelic face by my side, it was

more that I can express! He does look so beautiful in his shirt only, with his beautiful throat seen. We got up at ¼ p. 8. When I had laced I went to dearest Albert's room, and we breakfasted together. He had a black velvet jacket on, without any neckcloth on, and looked more beautiful than it is possible for me to say … At 12 I walked out with my precious Angel, all alone – so delightful, on the Terrace and new Walk, arm in arm!
>   QUEEN VICTORIA
>   *Journal*, 11 February 1840

Already the 2nd day since our marriage; his love and gentleness is beyond everything, and to kiss that dear soft cheek, to press my lips to his, is heavenly bliss. I feel a purer more unearthly feel than I ever did. Oh! was ever woman so blessed as I am.
>   QUEEN VICTORIA
>   *Journal*, 12 February 1840

My dearest Albert put on my stockings for me. I went in and saw him shave; a great delight for me.
>   QUEEN VICTORIA
>   *Journal*, 13 February 1840

> Purest Love's unwasting treasure,
> Constant faith, fair hope, long leisure,
> Days of ease, and nights of pleasure,
> Sacred Hymen! these are thine.
>   ALEXANDER POPE
>   *Tragedy of Brutus*

> Thus long in mutual bliss they lay embrac'd
> And their first Love continu'd to the last:
> One Sun-shine was their Life; no Cloud between;
> Nor ever was a kinder Couple seen.
> And so may all our Lives like their's be led;
> Heav'n send the Maids young Husbands, fresh in Bed:
> May Widows Wed as often as they can,
> And ever for the better change their Man.
>
> GEOFFREY CHAUCER
> *The Canterbury Tales*, The Wife of Bath's Tale

Let thy fountain be blessed: and rejoice with the wife of thy youth.

Let her be as the loving hind and pleasant roe; let her breasts satisfy thee at all times; and be thou ravished always with her love.

PROVERBS, 5:18–19

By an open window that looked on the brine through nodding roses, our young bridal pair were at breakfast, regaling worthily, both of them. Had the Scientific Humanist observed them, he could not have contested the fact, that as a couple who had set up to be father and mother of Britons, they were doing their duty. Files of egg-cups with disintegrated shells, bore witness to it, and they were still at work, hardly talking from rapidity of exercise ... Eating was the business of the hour, as I would have you to know it always will be where Cupid is in earnest.

GEORGE MEREDITH
The Ordeal of Richard Feverel

Honeymoon: The sugar on the bread of matrimony.
  OLIVER HERFORD
  Cupid's Cyclopedia, 1910

Christopher's answer was the answer of all young lovers not two days married, and it did seem to them both that they were actually in heaven.

Such happiness had not appeared to either of them possible, such a sudden revelation of what life could be, what life really was, when filled to the brim with only love ...

For three days in that happy, empty island, from whence the Easter tourists had departed and to which the summer tourists had not yet come, down by the sea, up in the woods, along through the buttercups, the sun shone on them by day and the stars by night, and there was no smallest falling off in ecstasy.

    ELIZABETH VON ARNIM
    Love

She could not accept that her present quiet life was the happiness she had dreamed of. And yet, these were, she realized, supposed to be the best days of her life. To experience the full delights of honeymoon days, it was probably necessary to go off to countries with resonant names, where the days could be passed in languorous pleasures! ... It seemed to her that certain places on earth surely produce happiness.

    GUSTAVE FLAUBERT
    Madame Bovary

Both were shocked at their mutual situation – that each should have betrayed anger towards the other. If they had been at home, settled at Lowick in ordinary life among their neighbours, the clash would have been less embarrassing: but on a wedding journey the express object of which is to isolate two people on the ground that they are all the world to each other, the sense of disagreement is, to say the least, confounding and stultifying.
GEORGE ELIOT
Middlemarch

Twin beds for a while until he read that they were out. He got a King-size monstrosity with a Scandinavian head-board. That finished my tranquillity.
EDNA O'BRIEN
Girls in Their Married Bliss

Halcyon Days

His honeymoon had been wonderful, but a fortnight is enough ... Here they were, he and she, entering into the joys, the varied joys of married life, with him, the male, girding up his loins in the morning and going forth to labour until the evening, as men from time immemorial had girded themselves and gone forth, and coming back at night to his nest and his mate. And this after all was better in the long run than a honeymoon, just as real good bread and butter was better than everlasting cake.
ELIZABETH VON ARNIM
Love

No happiness is like unto it, no love so great as that of man and wife, no such comfort as a sweet wife.
ROBERT BURTON
Anatomy of Melancholy

A happy marriage is a long conversation which always seems too short.
ANDRÉ MAUROIS
Memories

When Fred was riding home on winter evenings he had a pleasant vision beforehand of the bright hearth in the wainscoted parlour, and was sorry for other men who could not have Mary for their wife.
GEORGE ELIOT
Middlemarch

'I positively sometimes can't believe it,' said Traddles. 'Then, our pleasures! Dear me, they are inexpensive, but they are quite wonderful! When we are at home here of an evening, and shut the outer door, and draw those curtains – which she made – where could we be more snug? When it's fine, and we go out for a walk in the evening, the streets abound in enjoyment for us. We look into the glittering windows of the jewellers' shops; and I show Sophy which of the diamond-eyed serpents, coiled up on white satin rising grounds, I would give her if I could afford it; and Sophy shows me which of the gold watches … and all sorts of things, she would buy for me if *she* could afford it … Then, when we stroll into the squares and great streets, and see a house to let, sometimes we look up at it, and say, how would *that* do, if I was made a judge? And we parcel it out – such a room for us, such rooms for the girls, and so forth; until we settle to our satisfaction that it would do, or it wouldn't do, as the case may be. Sometimes, we go at half-price to the pit of the theatre – the very smell of which is cheap, in my opinion, at the money – and there we thoroughly enjoy the play: which Sophy believes every word of, and so do I. In walking home, perhaps we buy a little bit of something at a cook's-shop, or a little lobster at the fishmonger's, and bring it here, and make a splendid supper, chatting about what we have seen. Now, you know, Copperfield, if I was Lord Chancellor, we couldn't do this.'

    CHARLES DICKENS
    David Copperfield

… the astonishing glass shade had fallen that interposes between married couples and the world.
    E.M. FORSTER
    Howard's End

The only thing wrong with marriage is not seeing enough of each other.
>   EARL RUSSELL

I have not spent a single day without loving you; I have not spent a single night without wishing you were in my arms; I have not drunk a single cup of tea without cursing the glory and the ambition which keep me away from you, soul of my life. In the midst of my duties, at the head of the troops or as I go round the camps, my adorable Josephine is alone in my heart, and fills my thoughts. If I am going away from you with the speed of the Rhône torrent, it is so that I can see you again all the sooner. If I get up to do some work in the middle of the night, it is so that your arrival can be brought forward by a few days. And yet, in your letter of the 23rd and 26th Ventôse, you call me *vous*. *Vous* ... the same to you! Ah you wretch, how could you write this? Your letter is so cold! And then, it is four days from the 23rd to the 26th – what were you doing in that time if you were not writing to your husband?
>   NAPOLEON BONAPARTE
>   in a letter to his wife Josephine, 10 Germinal 1796, from Nice

My wife, what is the meaning of this? Why have I had no letter from you for two days?
>   ANTON CHEKHOV
>   in a letter to his wife Olga Knipper, 9 September 1901, from Yalta

Every hour makes me more impatient to hear from you, and everything I hear stir, I think brings me a letter. I shall not go about to excuse myself. I know 'tis a folly to a great degree to be so uneasy as I am at present, when I have no reason to apprehend any ill

cause ... I have stayed until I am asleep, in hopes; but they are vain, and I must once more go to bed, and wish to be waked with a letter from you, – which I shall at last get, I hope ... Adieu! do but love me and I can bear anything.
>QUEEN MARY II
>in a letter to William III, from Whitehall in July 1690

My dear dear life

If I shoud begin to tel you all the uneasynes & pain I have been in ever since you left me, and how much I long to see you again, it woud take more time to read than I hope you disine to stay; for endeed, my dear, tis more than I can bear to breath without you: (I cant call it liveing, for thats not posable for ye body to do when the soul is absent.) ... Tho' it was so late before I went to bed, I coud not go to sleep tel I had spent some time in washing your pillow with my tears, & kissing every part of it, for fear of missing that where your dear head had lain. I ris this morning by 8 a clock, thinking bed was the uneasyest place I coud meet with ... O dear, dear life, the pain I feel is not be expressd; I want more sand to dry my tears than ink upon this papar.
>ELIZABETH HERVEY
>in one of her numerous letters to her husband John Hervey, 25 April 1696, after about a year of marriage; *The Letter-Books of John Hervey*

Our state cannot be sever'd; we are one,
One flesh; to lose thee were to lose myself.
>JOHN MILTON
>*Paradise Lost*

Dearest Little Wife

... If I were to tell you everything I do with your dear portrait, you would laugh a good deal. For instance, whenever I take it out of its case, I say '*Gruess dich Gott, Stanzerl*! – *Gruess dich Gott, Spitzbub* – *Krollerballer* – *Spitzignas* – *Bagatellerl* – *schluck und druck*.' And when I put it back, I lower it slowly, and say at the same time *hu-hu-hu-hu*! with all the emphasis which this word of so many meanings requires, and finally, quickly, 'Good night, little mouse, sleep tight.' Now really, I believe I have written down something quite too stupid, for the world at least; but for us, who love each other so very much, it is not stupid at all.

    WOLFGANG AMADEUS MOZART
    in a letter to his wife Constanza, 13 April 1789

Editor's note: An approximate translation of Mozart's endearments is 'Hello there, Connie! Hello, naughty thing, bundle of trouble, snub-nose, little rascal.'

Oh that I were with you, or rather you with me here. The beds are so small that we should be forced to lie inside each other, and the weather is so hot that you might walk about naked all day, as well as night – *cela va sans dire*! Oh, those naked nights at Chelsea! When will they come again? I kiss both locks of hair every time I open my desk – but the little curly one seems to bring me nearer to you.

    CHARLES KINGSLEY
    in a letter to his wife Fanny, 24 July 1857

Intimations

Ev'n in the happiest choice, where fav'ring heaven
Has equal love and easy fortune giv'n, –
Think not, the husband gain'd, that all is done;
The prize of happiness must still be won:
And, oft, the careless find it to their cost,
The lover in the husband may be lost;
The graces might alone his heart allure;
They and the virtues, meeting, must secure.
    GEORGE LYTTELTON
    Advice to a Lady

A husband is what is left of the lover after the nerve has been extracted.
    HELEN ROWLAND
    The Rubaiyat of a Bachelor

Come, Madam, come, all rest my powers defie,
Until I labour, I in labour lie.
The foe oft-times having the foe in sight,
Is tir'd with standing though he never fight.
Off with that girdle, like heavens Zone glittering,
But a far fairer world incompassing ...
Licence my roaving hands, and let them go,
Before, behind, between, above, below.
    JOHN DONNE
    'Going to Bed'

There's sex, but it's not what you think. Marvellous for the first fortnight. Then every Wednesday, if there isn't a good late night concert on the third.
    MALCOLM BRADBURY
    Love on a Gunboat

Impossible for any one to conceive the torments of his nights in bed with his beloved one and estranged from her. That turning of backs, that cold space between their two unhappy bodies ...
    ELIZABETH VON ARNIM
    Love

Husbands are like fires – they go out when unattended.
    ZSA ZSA GABOR
    in *Newsweek*, 1960

Natasha paid no attention to the golden rule laid down by intelligent people, especially the French, that a young girl who gets married must not let herself go or throw away her talents, and should take even greater care of her appearance than before, so as to be more attractive than ever to her husband.
LEO TOLSTOY
War and Peace

All the world feels that a man when married acquires some of the attributes of an old woman – he becomes, to a certain extent, a motherly sort of being; he acquires a conversance with women's ways and women's wants, and loses the wilder and offensive sparks of his virility.
ANTHONY TROLLOPE

'You mustn't suppose for a moment, Fred,' she faltered, presently 'that I don't prefer my quiet evenings at home with you to anything else in the world, for I do; but – but don't you think that if we were never to go anywhere people would forget us, and we should be apt to grow dull and rusty? Were it not that I feel as if we owed it to ourselves to go about occasionally, I shouldn't mention the fact that, while you are at your office, I sometimes never speak to anybody for days at a time excepting baby and the servants.'
ROBERT GRANT
The Reflections of a Married Man, 1892

I drifted aimlessly from house to house, nursing the scarcely concealed consciousness that I would infinitely rather be at my own fireside with the wife of my bosom, than gallivanting in the gay world. In talking to the unmarried girls, I laboured under the dread that I was obstructing pre-matrimonial billing and cooing, and I found the average married woman of Josephine's age complacently ruminant as a milch cow, and disposed to enthusiasm only at the mention of her husband's name.
ROBERT GRANT
The Reflections of a Married Man, 1892

'Oh, William!' she cried imploringly ... 'Please! Please don't be so dreadfully stuffy and – tragic. You're always saying or looking or hinting that I've changed. Just because I've got to know really congenial people, and go about more, and am frightfully keen on – on everything, you behave as though I'd' – Isabel tossed back her hair and laughed – 'killed our love or something.'
KATHERINE MANSFIELD
Marriage à la Mode

I had business to occupy the whole of my time, Sundays and week-days, except sleeping hours; but I used to make time to assist her in the taking care of her baby, and in all sorts of things: get up, light her fire, boil her tea-kettle, carry her up warm water in cold weather, take the child while she dressed herself and got the breakfast ready, then breakfast, get her in water and wood for the day, then dress myself neatly, and sally forth to my business. The moment that was over I used to hasten back to her again; and I no more thought of spending a moment away from her, unless business compelled me, than I thought of quitting the country and going to sea.

WILLIAM COBBETT
his early married days, described in *Advice to Young Men and (Incidentally) to Young Women*, 1829

It remains an astonishing and tragic fact that *so* large a proportion of marriages lose their early bloom and are to some extent unhappy.... There are tragically few which approach even humanly attainable joy. Many of those considered by the world, by the relatives, *even by the loved and loving partner*, to be perfectly happy marriages, are secretly shadowed by the more sensitive of the pair.

    MARIE STOPES
    Married Love, 1918

'Do you feel,' she said softly, 'that you really know me now? But really, really know *me*?'

It was too much for George. Know his Fanny? He gave a broad, childish grin. 'I should jolly well think I do,' he said emphatically. 'Why, what's up?'

Fanny felt he hadn't quite understood. She went on quickly: 'What I mean is this. So often people, even when they love each other, don't seem to – to – it's so hard to say – know each other perfectly. They don't seem to want to. And I think that's awful. They misunderstand each other about the most important things of all.' Fanny looked horrified. 'George, we couldn't do that, could we? We never could.'

    KATHERINE MANSFIELD
    Honeymoon

'But what is it, Margaret?' he repeated. 'Have I done something?'

Then she said, dropping her voice, looking away from him:

'I thought you loved me no longer.'

His agitation increased. Loved her no longer, when he worshipped her? Loved her no longer when only last night ...? But now his old trouble, that he could never find words to express himself, attacked him.

'Love you?' he stammered. 'But, Margaret, I – I ... I could not love anyone more,' he ended, looking at her.

'No – I am sure. Of course. But perhaps it has been a great mistake. I am not handsome. I am not clever. This is your world and not mine ...' Then she burst out with a sudden cry, a note in her voice that he had never heard before. 'Oh, Adam, I have been so lonely!'

The shock to him then was one of the worst of his life. He had taken everything for granted. He had gone quietly on, troubled about his work and his feeble achievement in it, troubled at the state of the world and the general unhappiness, but sure always of two things – his love for Margaret and his mother, and their love for him. These were so sure that he never dreamed that they needed expression. Like so many other Englishmen he lived in a man's world where expression of feeling was something too foreign to be decent.

    HUGH WALPOLE
    The Herries Chronicle

And what then? For she felt that he was still looking at her, but that his look had changed. He wanted something – wanted the thing she always found it so difficult to give him; wanted her to tell him that she loved him. And that, no, she could not do. He found talking so much easier than she did. He could say things – she never could. So naturally it was always he that said the things, and then for some reason he would mind this suddenly, and would reproach her. A heartless woman he called her; she never told him that she loved him. But it was not so – it was not so. It was only that she never could say what she felt.

    VIRGINIA WOOLF
    To the Lighthouse

'The great thing is to have lots of love *about*. I don't see,' she went on, 'at least I don't see here, though I did at home, that it matters who loves as long as somebody does. I was a stingy beast at home, and used to measure and count. I had a queer obsession about justice. As though justice mattered. As though justice can really be distinguished from vengeance. It's only love that's any good. At home I wouldn't love Mellersh unless he loved me back, exactly as much, absolute fairness. Did you ever. And as he didn't, neither did I, and the *aridity* of that house! The *aridity* ...'

    ELIZABETH VON ARNIM
    The Enchanted April

As her husband advanced up the path she had a sudden vision of their three years together. Those years were her whole life; everything before them had been colorless and unconscious, like the blind life of the plant before it reaches the surface of the soil.

The years had not been exactly what she had dreamed; but if they had taken away certain illusions they had left richer realities in their stead. She understood now that she had gradually adjusted herself to the new image of her husband as he was, as he would always be. He was not the hero of her dreams, but he was the man she loved, and who had loved her. For she saw now, in this last wide flash of pity and initiation, that, as a comely marble may be made out of worthless scraps of mortar, glass, and pebbles, so out of mean mixed substances may be fashioned a love that will bear the stress of life.
 EDITH WHARTON
 Tales of Men and Ghosts

Try all that ever you can to be patient and good-natured with your *povera piccola Gooda*, and then she loves you, and is ready to do anything on earth that you wish, to fly over the moon, if you bade her. But when the *signor della casa* has neither kind look nor word for me, what can I do but grow desperate, fret myself to fiddlestrings, and be a torment to society in every direction?
 JANE WELSH CARLYLE
 in a letter to her husband Thomas Carlyle, 26
 October 1835, after nine years of marriage

I am afraid, dear Edwin and Angelina, you expect too much from love. You think there is enough of your little hearts to feed this fierce, devouring passion for all your long lives. Ah, young folk! don't rely too much upon that unsteady flicker. It will dwindle and dwindle as the months roll on, and there is no replenishing the fuel. You will watch it die out in anger and disappointment. To each it will seem that it is the other who is growing colder … It is a cheerless

hour for you both, when the lamp of love has gone out, and the fire of affection is not yet lit, and you have to grope about in the cold raw dawn of life to kindle it.
>JEROME K. JEROME
>*The Idle Thoughts of an Idle Fellow*

To marry a woman you love and who loves you is to lay a wager with her as to who will stop loving the other first.
>ALFRED CAPUS
>*Notes et pensées*

She would have a baby with her husband, to make up for the absence of love, to locate love, to fix herself in a certain place, but she would not really love him.
>JOYCE CAROL OATES
>*Them*

Herries watched Mirabell as a cat watches a bird, and he watched out of love and terror lest at any moment she should escape.

Now most truly he was paying for all the infidelities of his long life. He knew in the depths of the bitterest truth what the anguish of unrequited love was. He was sixty-two years of age and had never yet known such burning desire of the flesh, burning because it was eternally unsatisfied. Night after night he might lie with Mirabell and do with her what he would, and night after night, when she slept, he would get up from bed and walk the house like a frantic ghost because she did not love him.
>HUGH WALPOLE
>*The Herries Chronicle*

'Do you know,' she said, 'that since you have become my husband, I love you less than when you were my lover? I do not want to be tormented, and particularly not given orders. What I want is to be free and do as I please. Take care not to push me to the limit.'
PROSPER MÉRIMÉE
Carmen

I know many married men, I even know a few happily married men, but I don't know one who wouldn't fall down the first open coal hole running after the first pretty girl who gave him a wink.
GEORGE JEAN NATHAN
American critic

The concern that some women show at the absence of their husbands does not arise from their not seeing them and being with them, but from the apprehension that their husbands are enjoying pleasures in which they do not participate.
MICHEL DE MONTAIGNE

Being a husband is a wholetime job. That is why so many husbands fail. They cannot give their entire attention to it.
ARNOLD BENNETT
The Title

Marriage is the only thing that affords a woman the pleasure of company and the perfect sensation of solitude at the same time.
HELEN ROWLAND
The Book of Diversion

I know nothing about sex, because I was always married.
   ZSA ZSA GABOR

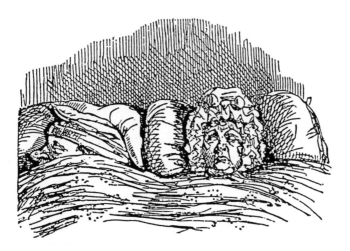

Why should such a foolish Marriage Vow
Which long ago was made,
Oblige us to each other now
When Passion is decay'd?
We lov'd, and we lov'd, as long as we cou'd,
Till our Love was lov'd out in us both:
But our Marriage is dead, when the Pleasure is
   fled:
'Twas Pleasure first made it an Oath.
   JOHN DRYDEN
   Marriage à la Mode

Rows

'Oh, you cruel, cruel boy, to say I am a disagreeable wife!' cried Dora.

'Now, my dear Dora, you must know that I never said that!'

'You said I wasn't comfortable!' cried Dora.

'I said the housekeeping was not comfortable!'

'It's exactly the same thing!' cried Dora. And she evidently thought so, for she wept most grievously.

CHARLES DICKENS
David Copperfield

I have your letter, wherein you let me know that the little dispute we have had is far from being a trouble to you; nevertheless, I assure you, any disturbance between us is the greatest affliction to me imaginable …

I love you better than the light of my eyes, or the life-blood in my heart; but when I have let you know that, you are also to understand that neither my sight shall be so far enchanted, nor my affection so much master of me, as to make me forget our common interest.

RICHARD STEELE
in a letter to his wife Mary, 12 August 1708

Sir Peter: … We shall now be the happiest couple –
Lady Teazle: And never differ again?
Sir Peter: No, never – though at the same time, indeed, my dear Lady Teazle, you must watch your temper very seriously; for in all our little quarrels, my dear, if you recollect, my love, you always began first.
Lady Teazle: I beg your pardon, my dear Sir Peter: indeed, you always gave the provocation.

Sir Peter: Now, see, my angel! take care – contradicting isn't the way to keep friends.
Lady Teazle: Then, don't you begin it, my love!
Sir Peter: There, now! you – you are going on. You don't perceive, my life, that you are just doing the very thing which you know always makes me angry.
>RICHARD SHERIDAN
>*The School for Scandal*

'Dora, my darling!'

'No, I am not your darling. Because you *must* be sorry that you married me, or else you wouldn't reason with me!' returned Dora.
>CHARLES DICKENS
>*David Copperfield*

'I left Sudbury one dark night – it was winter time – about nine o'clock; the rain poured in torrents, the wind howled among the trees that skirted the roadside, and I was obliged to proceed at a foot-pace, for I could hardly see my hand before me, it was so dark–'

'John,' interrupted Mrs Parsons, in a low, hollow voice, 'don't spill that gravy.'

'Fanny,' said Parsons impatiently, 'I wish you'd defer these domestic reproofs to some more suitable time. Really, my dear, these constant interruptions are very annoying.'

'My dear, I didn't interrupt you,' said Mrs Parsons.

'But, my dear, you *did* interrupt me,' remonstrated Mr Parsons.

'How very absurd you are, my love!'
   CHARLES DICKENS
   Sketches by Boz

'Dear me, Edmund, if you have anything to say, why don't you say it?'

Mr Sparkler might have replied with ingenuousness, 'My life, I have nothing to say.' But, as the repartee did not occur to him, he contented himself with coming in from the balcony and standing at the side of his wife's couch.
   CHARLES DICKENS
   Little Dorrit

Show me one couple unhappy merely on account of their limited circumstances, and I will show you ten who are wretched from other causes.
   SAMUEL TAYLOR COLERIDGE
   Table Talk, 10 June 1824

It helps in a pinch to be able to remind your bride that you gave up a throne for her.
> THE DUKE OF WINDSOR

Love is the coldest of critics.
> GEORGE WILLIAM CURTIS
> *Prue and I*

Quarrels are the dowry which married people bring one another.
> OVID
> *The Art of Love*

I am always wondering since I came here how I can, even in my angriest mood, talk about leaving you for good and all; for to be sure, if I were to leave you today on that *principle*, I should need absolutely to go back tomorrow *to see how you were taking it*.
> JANE WELSH CARLYLE
> in a letter to her husband Thomas Carlyle, 2 July 1844, from Liverpool

In marriage, as in war, it is permitted to take every advantage of the enemy.
> DOUGLAS JERROLD
> author of *Mrs Caudle's Curtain Lectures*

Marriage: a souvenir of love.
> HELEN ROWLAND
> *Reflections of a Bachelor Girl*, 1903

Getting divorced just because you don't love a man is almost as silly as getting married just because you do.
> ZSA ZSA GABOR

They say a parson first invented gunpowder, but one cannot believe it till one is married.
>DOUGLAS JERROLD

George: Total war?
Martha: Total.
>EDWARD ALBEE
>*Who's Afraid of Virginia Woolf?*

Divorce, n. A resumption of diplomatic relations and rectification of boundaries.
>AMBROSE BIERCE
>*The Enlarged Devil's Dictionary*

Affairs

What men call Gallantry, and the Gods adultery,
Is much more common when the climate's sultry.
LORD BYRON
Don Juan

The lover thinks more about how to get to his mistress than the husband thinks about keeping his wife in.
STENDHAL
La Chartreuse de Parme

Yesterday I received your two letters, dear heart; I thank you for them. But now I have to read the Riot Act to you a little. All you seem to think of these days is flirting – but listen to me: it is no longer the fashion, and is considered evidence of a bad upbringing. There is no sense in it. You are pleased that men run after you – congratulations! But even Praskaya Petrovna would have no trouble in getting the pack of unmarried idlers to run after her. When the trough is there, the pigs come up of their own accord.

ALEXANDER PUSHKIN
in a letter to his wife Natalya, from Boldino, 30 October 1833. He was later killed in a duel on her behalf.

I do not love you any more: on the contrary, I hate you ... You never write to me; you don't love your husband; you know the pleasure your letters give him, and yet you scribble barely six lines.

What are you doing all day, Madame? What important business prevents you from writing to your good husband? What affection stifles and displaces the love, the tender and constant love that you promised him? Who is this marvellous new lover who takes up all your time and is master of your days? ... Josephine, be careful: one of these nights, the doors will burst open and I'll be there.
NAPOLEON BONAPARTE
in a letter to Josephine, 13 November 1796

She manages very well but if I come away with a stiletto in my gizzard some fine afternoon, I shall not be astonished.

I can't make *him* out at all – he visits me frequently, and takes me out ... in a coach and *six* horses. The fact appears to be, that he is completely *governed* by her – for that matter, so am I. The people here don't know what to make of us, as he had the character of jealousy with all his wives – this is the third. He is the richest of the Ravennese, by their own account, but he is not popular among them. By the aid of a Priest, a Chambermaid, a young Negro-boy, and a female friend, we are enabled to carry on our unlawful loves, as far as they can well go, though generally with some peril, especially as the female friend and priest are at present out of town for some days, so that some of the precautions devolve upon the Maid and Negro.
LORD BYRON
describing his affair with Teresa Guiccioli, in a letter from Ravenna to Richard Belgrave Hoppner, 20 June 1819

She was imprudence itself; she made no attempt to keep her voice down, nor did Julien; and it was about two o'clock in the morning when they were interrupted by a violent knocking at the door. It was M de Rênal again.

'Open up quickly, there are burglars in the house!' he called out, 'their ladder has been found.'

'This is the end,' said Mme de Rênal, throwing herself into Julien's arms, 'He is going to kill us both; he does not really believe there are burglars. I will die in your arms, happier in death than I was in life.' And she did not even bother to answer her husband who was getting angry, but kissed Julien passionately.

'... I am going to jump into the courtyard by the dressing-room window, and get away through the garden ... Make a bundle of my clothes, and throw it down as soon as you can. In the meantime, let your husband break down the door. But no confessions, I forbid it. Better he should be suspicious rather than certain.'

'You'll kill yourself jumping,' was her only answer.

STENDHAL
Le Rouge et le noir

To warn her, Rodolphe would throw a handful of sand against the shutters. She would jump up immediately, but she often had to wait, for Charles liked nothing better than sitting and chatting by the fireside. Would he never move? She was consumed with impatience ...

At last, she was preparing for bed; then she would take a book and carry on reading quietly as though completely absorbed. Charles, who was now in bed, would call out to her: 'Come along, Emma, it's late.'

'I'm coming,' she would answer.

But as the candles dazzled him, he would turn to the wall and fall asleep. And then she made her escape, holding her breath, smiling and tremulous, in her night clothes.

Rodolphe had a greatcoat with him which he wrapped round her, and, putting his arm round her waist, he led her without a word to the bottom of the garden.

> GUSTAVE FLAUBERT
> *Madame Bovary*

'I am tired of killing all your lovers; you are the one I will kill next time.'

She looked at me intently with a wild look in her eye, and said: 'I have always known you would kill me one day … It is destiny.'

> PROSPER MÉRIMÉE
> *Carmen*

I am afraid of this love. I am so afraid – to let it go or to take it. I dare not take it; but to let it go and then afterwards to look back and remember what might have been – that makes it unendurable to live.

> CHARLES MORGAN
> *The Fountain*

The more civilized people become the less capable they seem of lifelong happiness with one partner.

> BERTRAND RUSSELL
> *Marriage and Morals*, 1929

I would have felt more pleasure at returning to her of my own free will without feeling that it was an obligation, that she was waiting for me with impatience, and without the thought of her unhappiness diluting the happiness I felt to see her again. Ellenore was still an intense pleasure in my life, but she was no longer an aim: she had become a tie.

> BENJAMIN CONSTANT
> *Adolphe*

She did not see enough of him, did not get enough of him, and felt with the acquired wisdom of her observations that too little was infinitely better than too much, that desire was in every way preferable to possession.
>   MARGARET DRABBLE
>   *Jerusalem the Golden*

I am not faithful, but I am attached.
>   GUNTER GRASS

He was a man of unwearied and prolific conjugal fidelity.
>   VICENTE BLASCO Y IBÁÑEZ
>   *Blood and Sand*

Partings

Yes! Farewell – farewell forever!
Thou thyself has fixed our doom,
Bade hope's fairest blossoms wither,
Ne'er again for me to bloom.
> ANNE ISABELLA MILBANKE
> 'Fare Thee Well' written to her husband Lord Byron, *c.* January 1816

There is in a long-lasting relationship something so profound! It becomes without our realizing it such an intimate part of our life. We take, from a distance, the decision to break it off; we await, with impatience we think, the moment to carry it out. But when the time comes, we are terrified at the prospect; and such is the waywardness of our miserable heart that we have terrible pangs at parting from those with whom we stayed without pleasure.
> BENJAMIN CONSTANT
> Adolphe

I do not love you, but I adore you for ever. I do not want you but I cannot live without you …
> GEORGE SAND
> in a letter to Alfred de Musset in 1834

I never want to see him again. It makes me too unhappy. But I shall need all my resolve to refuse to see him, because he is sure to ask it. He no longer loves me but is always tender and repentant after he has been cruel … He will think he is helping me but he is wrong, for I shall start loving him again and all my efforts in detaching myself from him will have been in vain.
> GEORGE SAND
> in a letter to her friend Sainte-Beuve in late 1834

Oh my God! what is there left of our great and beautiful passion? Neither love nor friendship. Oh my God!
>   GEORGE SAND
>   in a letter to Alfred de Musset in the winter of 1834–5

I never wanted but your heart. That gone, you have nothing more to give. Had I only poverty to fear, I should not shrink from life. Forgive me then, if I say, that I shall consider any direct or indirect attempt to supply my necessities, as an insult which I have not merited, and as rather done out of tenderness for your own reputation, than for me. Do not mistake me; I do not think that you value money, therefore I will not accept what you do not care for, though I do much less, because certain privations are not painful to me.
>   MARY WOLLSTONECRAFT
>   in a letter to Gilbert Imlay, written shortly before a suicide attempt, in 1795

> I hold it true, whate'er befall;
> I feel it, when I sorrow most;
> 'Tis better to have loved and lost
> Than never to have loved at all.
>   ALFRED, LORD TENNYSON
>   *In Memoriam*

We were like magnets, alternating pulling towards each other and inexorably pushing away.
>   ELIZABETH TAYLOR of her relationship with Richard Burton

I had been chaste for too long: two or three weeks.
>   ISABEL ALLENDE
>   explaining how she came to fall in love at first sight with her second husband

Maj: Oh, d---, I'd forgotten!
Em: Forgotten what?
Maj: The children. I ought to have told you. Do you mind children?
Em: Not in moderate quantities. How many have you got?
Maj: (*counting hurriedly on his fingers*): Five.
Em: Five!
Maj: (anxiously): Is that too many?
Em: It's rather a number. The worst of it is, I've some myself.
Maj: Many?
Em: Eight.
Maj: Eight in six years! Oh, Emily!
Em: Only four were my own. The other four were by my husband's first marriage. Still, that practically makes eight.
Maj: And eight and five make thirteen. We can't start our married life with thirteen children; it would be most unlucky.
>SAKI
>problems for Major Dumbarton and Mrs Emily Carewe the second time round, *The Baker's Dozen*

An ache of longing to see Virginia stole into her heart. One's children and new husbands – how difficult they were to mix comfortably.
>ELIZABETH VON ARNIM
>*Love*

Mature Love

I know as certainly as I live that I have been for twelve years as passionate a lover as ever woman was, and hope to be so one twelve years more.
RACHEL RUSSELL
in a letter to her husband Lord William Russell in 1682

It was the generosity of delight
that first we learned in a sparsely-furnished flat
clothed in our lovers' nakedness. By night
we timidly entered what we marvelled at,

ranging the flesh's compass. But by day
we fell together, fierce with awkwardness
that window-light and scattered clothing lay
impassive round such urgent happiness.

Now, children, years and many rooms away,
and tired with experience, we climb the stairs
to our well-furnished room; undress, and say
familiar words for love; and from the cares

that back us, turn together and once more seek
the warmth of wonder each to the other meant
so strong ago, and with known bodies speak
the unutterable language of content.
MAURICE LINDSAY
'Love's Anniversaries (for Joyce)', 1964

Now, as to your ladyship, when I think fit to look at you, to hear you, to touch you, gives delight in a greater degree than any other creature can bestow; and indeed it is not virtue, but good sense and wise choice to be constant to you. You did well not to dwell upon one circumstance in your letter; for which I am in good health, and I thank God I am at this present writing, it awakes wishes too warmly to be well borne when you are at so great a distance.
RICHARD STEELE
in a letter to his wife Mary, 11 July 1717

… I shall not be out of apprehension until I may have the happiness of thy company. For, indeed, I think it not the least of my misfortunes that for my sake thou hast run so much hazard; in which thou hast expressed so much love to me that I confess it is impossible to repay by anything I can do, much less by words. But my heart being full of affection of thee, admiration of thee, and impatient passion of gratitude to thee, I could not but say something, leaving the rest to be read by thee out of thine own noble heart.
KING CHARLES I
in a letter to Queen Henrietta Maria, who had sought refuge in France, 13 February 1643

My own dearest and best, – We parted manfully and womanfully as we ought. I drank only half a bottle of the Rhine wine, and only the half of that, ere I fell asleep on the sofa, which lasted two hours. It was the reaction, for your going tired me more than I cared to show. Then I drank the other half, and as that did not do, I went and retraced our walk in the park, and sat down in *the same seat*, and felt happier and better. Have you not a romantic old husband?
THOMAS HOOD
in a letter to his wife (Reynolds' sister)

Every day every hour every moment makes me feel more deeply how blessed we are in each other, how purely how faithfully how ardently, and how tenderly we love each other; I put this last word last because, though I am persuaded that a deep affection is not uncommon in married life, yet I am confident that a lively, gushing, thought-employing, spirit-stirring, passion of love, is very rare even among good people … O Mary I love you with a passion of love which grows till I tremble to think of its strength …
>WILLIAM WORDSWORTH
>in a letter to his wife Mary, 11 August 1810, after eight years of marriage

As the years pass I *hate* being parted from him even for an hour or so; I feel only half a person by myself, with one arm, one leg and half a face.
>FRANCES PARTRIDGE
>of her husband Ralph Partridge, *Everything to Lose: Diaries 1945-1960*

My dear dear Angell will see by my last letter how much I reckond upon your coming, therefore it will be needless to tell you how great the disappointment was, nor indeed I coud not if I woud. From eleven a clock I began to listen to every coach that came near the door; I believe my maids and I were a hundred times at the window; my aunts came to see me, but I believe they were quite tired of me, for every question they asked me was answerd with – I begin to think he wont come, it grows so late.
>ELIZABETH HERVEY, LADY BRISTOL
>in a letter to her husband John Hervey, 18 April 1713, after 18 years of marriage
>*The Letter-Books of John Hervey*

To tell you that for the last nine years I love you more each day, that my love is like a tree which every year grows a new root in the soil, and a new branch in the sky; to tell you that I dream of you when I am not thinking of you; ... to tell you that you are my joy, my hope, my purpose, my reward, my pride; to tell you all that, my beloved, is to tell you things that you know already, that I have told you a hundred times; but it is a joy for me to repeat it once more as it will be for you (will it not?) to hear it one more time.
  VICTOR HUGO
  in a letter to Juliette Drouet, 21 May 1842

I can state with complete truth that everything remains the same in my heart as the night I first became yours. These thirty years of love have passed like one day of uninterrupted adoration, ... I smile upon you, bless you, adore you.
  JULIETTE DROUET
  in a letter to Victor Hugo, 17 February 1863

Dearest adored one, I do not know where I may be this time next year, but I am proud and happy to sign my life certificate for 1883 with this one word: I love you.
  JULIETTE DROUET
  in her last letter to Victor Hugo, 1 January 1883

The heart becomes saturated with love as with a divine salt which preserves it; hence the steadfast attachment of those who have loved each other from the dawn of life, and the freshness of old loves which still endure. Love can become embalmed. Daphnis

and Chloe become Philemon and Baucis. Old age is then like evening resembling the dawn.
> VICTOR HUGO
> *L'Homme qui rit*

Dawn love is silver,
Wait for the west:
Old love is gold love –
Old love is best.
> KATHERINE LEE BATES
> 'For a Golden Wedding'

Doe you remember Arme and the little house there? shall wee goe thither? that is next to being out of the worlde. there wee might live like Baucis and Philemon, grow old together in our little Cottage and for our Charrity to some shipwrakt stranger obtaine the blessing of dyeing both at the same time. how idly I talk! tis because the storry pleases me, none in Ovide soe much. I remember I cryed when I read it, mee thought they were the perfectest characters of a contented marriage where Piety and love were all there wealth.
> DOROTHY OSBORNE
> in a letter to William Temple, 13 January 1653/4

John Anderson, my jo, John,
When we were first acquent;
Your locks were like the raven,
Your bonie brow was brent;
But now your brow is beld, John,
Your locks are like the snow;
But blessings on your frosty pow,
John Anderson, my jo.
John Anderson, my jo, John,
We clamb the hill thegither;

And mony a cantie day, John,
We've had wi' ane anither:
Now we maun totter down, John,
And hand in hand we'll go,
And sleep thegither at the foot,
John Anderson, my jo.
   ROBERT BURNS
   'John Anderson, My Jo'

Memories

The memory of a love that has been cut short by death remains still fragrant though enfeebled, but no recollection of its past can keep sweet a love that has dried up and withered through accidents of time and life.
    SAMUEL BUTLER
    Note-Books

Bereavement is a universal and integral part of our experience of love. It follows marriage as normally as marriage follows courtship or as autumn follows summer.
    C.S. LEWIS
    A Grief Observed

What is not connected with her to me? and what does not recall her? I cannot look down to this floor, but her features are shaped on the flags! In every cloud, in every tree – filling the air at night, and caught by glimpses in every object, by day I am surrounded with her image! ... The entire world is a dreadful collection of memoranda that she did exist, and that I have lost her!
    EMILY BRONTË
    Heathcliff is haunted, *Wuthering Heights*

But he [Linton] was too good to be thoroughly unhappy long. *He* didn't pray for Catherine's soul to haunt him: Time brought resignation, and a melancholy sweeter than common joy. He recalled her memory with ardent, tender love, and hopeful aspiring to the better world, where, he doubted not, she was gone.
    EMILY BRONTË
    Wuthering Heights

He stood a few minutes reading over and over again the words on the tombstone, as if to assure himself that all the happy and unhappy past was a reality. For love is frightened at the intervals of insensibility and callousness that encroach by little and little on the dominion of grief, and it makes efforts to recall the keenness of the first anguish.

Gradually, as his eye dwelt on the words, 'Amelia, the beloved wife', the waves of feeling swelled within his soul, and he threw himself on the grave, clasping it with his arms, and kissing the cold turf.

'Milly, Milly, dost thou hear me? I didn't love thee enough – I wasn't tender enough to thee – but I think of it all now.'
GEORGE ELIOT
The Sad Fortunes of the Revd Amos Barton, Scenes of Clerical Life

My dearest dust, could not thy hasty day
Afford thy drowszy patience leave to stay
One hower longer: so that we might either
Sate up, or gone to bedd together?
But since thy finisht labor hath possest
Thy weary limbs with early rest,
Enjoy it sweetly: and thy widdowe bride
Shall soone repose her by thy slumbring side.
Whose business, now, is only to prepare
My nightly dress, and call to prayre:
Mine eyes wax heavy and ye day growes old.
The dew falls thick, my belovd growes cold.
Draw, draw ye closed curtaynes: and make roome:
My deare, my dearest dust; I come, I come.
LADY CATHERINE DYER
epitaph on the monument erected by her to Sir William Dyer, in a Bedfordshire parish church, in 1641

Elizabeth was fifty-four and as beautiful now as she had been at twenty ... She had the air of remoteness that had been hers ever since John's death. She was not priggish nor superior in this. She joined in everything that went on, laughed, sang, played games ... but nothing could bring her into the real current of life that the others shared. She loved her son, she loved Judith, she loved Jane, but even they, even Benjamin, were shades compared with John. When he was killed she received a blow that was mortal.
>HUGH WALPOLE
>*The Herries Chronicle*

He first deceased; she for a little tried
To live without him, liked it not, and died.
>SIR HENRY WOTTON
>'Upon the Death of Sir Albert Morton's Wife',
>1651

I'm devastated. I don't know how I'm going to live without her. The only consolation is knowing that we will soon be reunited. Our love will continue in heaven.
>JAMES STEWART
>on losing his wife Gloria Swanson in February 1994 after 45 years of marriage

Regrets

When you are old and grey and full of sleep,
And nodding by the fire, take down this book,
And slowly read, and dream of the soft look
Your eyes had once, and of their shadows deep;

How many loved your moments of glad grace,
And loved your beauty with love false or true,
But one man loved the pilgrim soul in you,
And loved the sorrows of your changing face;

And bending down beside the glowing bars,
Murmur, a little sadly, how Love fled
And paced upon the mountains overhead
And hid his face amid a crowd of stars.
   W.B. YEATS
   'When You Are Old'

She sighed; then, after a long silence: 'No matter, we will have loved each other well.'
  'Without belonging to each other, however!'
  'Perhaps that is for the best,' she said again.
  'No, no! What happiness would have been ours!'
  'Oh! I can believe it, with a love like ours!'
   GUSTAVE FLAUBERT
   L'Education sentimentale

Janet's was a nature in which hatred and revenge could find no place; the long bitter years drew half their bitterness from her ever-living remembrance of the too short years of love that went before; and the thought that her husband would ever put her hand to his lips again, and recall the days when they sat on the grass together, and he laid scarlet poppies on her black hair, and called her his gypsy queen, seemed to send a tide of loving oblivion over all the harsh and stony space they had traversed since.
GEORGE ELIOT
Janet's Repentance, Scenes of Clerical Life

Something he knew he had missed: the flower of life. But he thought of it now as a thing so unattainable and improbable that to have repined would have been like despairing because one had not drawn the first prize in a lottery. There were a hundred million tickets in *his* lottery, and there was only one prize; the chances had been too decidedly against him. When he thought of Ellen Olenska it was abstractly, serenely, as one might think of some imaginary beloved in a book or a picture: she had become the composite vision of all that he had missed. That vision, faint and tenuous as it was, had kept him from thinking of other women. He had been what was called a faithful husband; and when May had suddenly died … he had honestly mourned her. Their long years together had shown him that it did not so much matter if marriage was a dull duty, as long as it kept the dignity of a duty: lapsing from that, it became a mere battle of ugly appetites.
EDITH WHARTON
The Age of Innocence

Wisdom

One makes mistakes: that is life. But it is never quite a mistake to have loved.
> ROMAIN ROLLAND
> *Summer*

'Tis impossible to love and be wise.
> FRANCIS BACON
> *Essays*: 'Of Love'

There is no remedy for love but to love more.
> HENRY D. THOREAU
> *Journal*, 25 July 1839

Love is the loadstone of love.
> OLD ENGLISH PROVERB

Why is it better to love than to be loved? It is surer.
> SACHA GUITRY

The essence of love is creative companionship, the fulfilment of one life by another.
> JOHN ERSKINE
> *The Complete Life*

What she saw ... was that love has to learn to let go, that love if it is real always does let go, makes no claims, sets free, is content to love without being loved ...
> ELIZABETH VON ARNIM
> *Love*

Let me not to the marriage of true mindes
Admit impediments, love is not love
Which alters when it alteration findes,
Or bends with the remover to remove.
O no, it is an ever fixed marke
That lookes on tempests and is never shaken;
    WILLIAM SHAKESPEARE

True love is like a ghost; everybody talks about it but few have seen it.
    LA ROCHEFOUCAULD
    Maximes

Let there be spaces in your togetherness …
Love one another, but make not a bond of love:
Let it rather be a moving sea between the shores of your souls.
Fill each other's cup but drink not from one cup.
    KAHLIL GIBRAN
    The Prophet

Come my Celia, let us prove,
While we may, the sports of love;
Time will not be ours, for ever:
He, at length, our good will sever.
Spend not then his guifts in vaine.
Sunnes, that set, may rise againe:
But if once we loose this light,
'Tis, with us, perpetuall night.
Why should we deferre our joyes? …
   BEN JONSON
   'To Celia'

Breathless, we flung us on the windy hill,
Laughed in the sun, and kissed the lovely grass.
You said, 'Through glory and ecstasy we pass;
Wind, sun, and earth remain, the birds sing still,
When we are old, are old …' 'And when we die
All's over that is ours; and life burns on
Through other lovers, other lips,' said I,
'Heart of my heart, our heaven is now, is won!'
   RUPERT BROOKE
   'The Hill'

Envoi

If you would be loved, love and be lovable.
BENJAMIN FRANKLIN

Index

Abelard, Peter, 86
Addison, Joseph, 99
Ade, George, 125
Albee, Edward, 164
Allen, Woody, 15
Allende, Isabel, 173
Anderson, Sherwood, 24
Aristotle, 88
Arnim, Elizabeth von, 49, 60, 140, 143, 149, 155, 173, 185
Ashford, Daisy, 111
Aubrey, John, 117
Auchincloss, Louis, 1
Austen, Jane, 26, 28, 43, 46, 66, 94, 113, 121, 130

Bacon, Francis, 185
Bagehot, Walter, 25
Balzac, Honoré de, 11, 24
Barry, Lynda, 37
Bates, Katherine Lee, 178
Beecher, Henry Ward, 11
Behn, Aphra, 48, 59, 72, 74, 82
Behrman, S.N., 44
Bennett, Arnold, 158
Bierce, Ambrose, 12, 20, 74, 164

Boccaccio, 89
Bonaparte, Lucien, 50
Bonaparte, Napoleon, 73, 145, 167
Boswell, James, 86, 87, 100, 116
Bradbury, Malcolm, 148
Braddon, Mary Elizabeth, 14
Braine, John, 84
Brews, Margery, 70
Brontë, Charlotte, 132
Brontë, Emily, 33, 50, 77, 180
Brooke, Rupert, 187
Brown, Rita Mae, 17
Browning, Elizabeth Barrett, 54
Burney, Fanny, 113
Burns, Robert, 53, 96, 105, 120, 179
Burton, Robert, 100, 143
Butler, Samuel, 11, 15, 30, 96, 102, 180
Byron, Lord, 25, 39, 51, 54, 92, 165, 167

Callas, Maria, 18
Capus, Alfred, 157

Carlyle, Jane Welsh, 126, 156, 163
Carlyle, Thomas, 126
Carpenter, Charlotte, 122
Casanova, Giacomo, 28, 83, 85, 86, 93
Catherine II of Russia, 86
Charles I, King, 175
Chaucer, Geoffrey, 9, 19, 138
Chekhov, Anton, 145
Chesterton, G.K., 18
Chevalier, Maurice, 23
Churchill, Jennie Jerome, 16
Clare, John, 36
Cleland, John, 37, 84, 85, 90
Cobbett, William, 104, 152
Coleridge, Samuel Taylor, 162
Colette, 127
Congreve, William, 122
Constant, Benjamin, 49, 50, 79, 87, 96, 170, 171
Coward, Noel, 94
Crawford, F. Marion, 28
Curtis, George William, 163

Daniels, Paul, 87
Defoe, Daniel, 45
Dell, Floyd, 31
Dickens, Charles, 32, 38, 44, 45, 77, 78, 107, 109, 110, 115, 133, 134, 144, 160, 161, 162
Dickinson, Emily, 62
Dietrich, Marlene, 15
Disraeli, Benjamin, 41, 43, 49, 62, 99, 119
Donne, John, 54, 85, 91, 148
Drabble, Margaret, 170
Dreikurs, Dr Rudolf, 102
Dressler, Marie, 27
Drouet, Juliette, 71, 74, 90, 177
Dryden, John, 159
Dumas, Alexandre, 61
Dyer, Lady Catherine, 181

Eden, Emily, 130
Edward VIII, Duke of Windsor, 73, 163
Eliot, George, 80, 94, 98, 112, 121, 141, 143, 181, 184
Erasmus, 88
Erskine, John, 32, 185

Faraday, Michael, 68
Ferrier, Susan, 72
Fielding, Henry, 20, 28, 80
Firkins, Oscar W., 55
Fitzgerald, F. Scott, 134
Flaubert, Gustave, 36, 140, 169, 183
Fleming, Marjory, 13
Forster, E.M., 144
Franklin, Benjamin, 23, 188
Freud, Sigmund, 87, 93
Fromm, Erich, 18
Frost, Robert, 20
Fuller, Margaret, 30

Gabor, Zsa Zsa, 135, 149, 159, 163
Gardner, Ring, 38
Gay, John, 59
Géraldy, Paul, 24
Gibran, Kahlil, 186
Gilbert, W.S., 16
Giovanni, Nikki, 20
Godolphin, Sidney, 76
Goethe, 21
Goldman, Emma, 18
Grant, Cary, 89
Grant, Robert, 151
Grass, Gunter, 170
Graves, Robert, 12
Greer, Germaine, 15
Greville, Frances, 95
Guitry, Sacha, 185

Hardy, Thomas, 58, 114
Haywood, Eliza, 39
Hecht, Ben, 88
Heine, Heinrich, 129
Heller, Joseph, 88
Héloise, 67, 98
Hemingway, Ernest, 84
Henry VIII, King, 69, 70
Herford, Oliver, 51, 56, 59, 66, 128, 139
Herrick, Robert, 136
Hervey, Elizabeth, Lady Bristol, 146, 176
Hervey, Thomas, 68
Hogg, James, 52
Holmes, Oliver Wendell, 56
Hood, Thomas, 175
Howard, Joy, 37

Howe, E.W., 27
Hugo, Victor, 53, 71, 76, 177, 178

Ibáñez, Vicente Blasco Y, 170
Irving, Washington, 46
Jackson, Helen Hunt, 54
James, Henry, 48, 77
Jerome, Jerome K., 34, 41, 157
Jerrold, Douglas, 135, 163, 164
Johnson, Samuel, 104
Jones, Franklin P., 14
Jonson, Ben, 187

Kilvert, Revd Francis, 38, 60, 62
King, Alexander, 24, 117
Kingsley, Charles, 12, 147
Kipling, Rudyard, 58

La Bruyère, 96
Laclos, Choderlos de, 87
La Fayette, Mme de, 81
La Rochefoucauld, 101, 186
Lawrence, D.H., 15
Leacock, Stephen, 104
Leatherbarrow, Revd Ron, 134
Lebowitz, Fran, 21
Lee, Laurie, 33
Lerner, Max, 20
Lespinasse, Julie de, 74
Leszcynski, Stanislaus, King of Poland, 101
Lewis, C.S., 180
Lindsay, Maurice, 174
Longfellow, Henry Wadsworth, 38
Luce, Clare Boothe, 27
Lyttelton, George, 36, 148
Magnani, Anna, 16
Mannes, Marya, 39
Mansfield, Katherine, 119, 151, 153
Mary II, Queen, 146
Maugham, W. Somerset, 15
Maupassant, Guy de, 18
Maurois, André, 75, 143
May, Rollo, 30
Mencken, H.L., 21
Meredith, George, 20, 49, 138
Mérimée, Prosper, 158, 169

Milbanke, Anne Isabella, 171
Millay, Edna St Vincent, 98
Miller, Henry, 74
Milton, John, 146
Mirren, Helen, 41
Mitford, Nancy, 36
Molière, 81
Molton, Louise, 98
Montagu, Lady Mary Wortley, 126
Montaigne, Michel de, 158
Montgomerie, Margaret, 116
Moore, Thomas, 70
Morgan, Charles, 169
Mozart, Wolfgang Amadeus, 147
Murdoch, Iris, 92
Murphy, Robert C., 18
Musset, Alfred de, 11, 14, 90, 92

Nash, Ogden, 44
Nathan, George Jean, 158
Nelson, Horatio, 69
Neuberger, Rabbi Julia, 103
Nicolson, Harold, 54

Oates, Joyce Carol, 157
O'Brien, Edna, 141
Orczy, Baroness, 48
Osborne, Dorothy, 67, 78, 102, 178
Ovid, 11, 163
Owen, Dr David, 16

Parker, Dorothy, 14, 95
Partridge, Frances, 176
Pavese, Cesare, 28
Peacock, Thomas Love, 105
Perelman, S.J., 15
Piggy, Miss, 97
Pisan, Christine de, 29
Pope, Alexander, 137
Powys, John Cowper, 74
Prévost, Abbé, 35
Proust, Marcel, 24
Pushkin, Alexander, 166

Raleigh, Sir Walter, 12
Ray, John, 44, 135
Rayner, Claire, 103

Richardson, Frank, 106
Rilke, Rainer Maria, 19
Rolland, Romain, 185
Rossetti, Christina, 60
Rowland, Helen, 25, 56, 105, 148, 158, 163
Russell, Bertrand, 103, 169
Russell, Earl, 145
Russell, Rachel, 174
Rutherford, Mark, 78

Saint-Exupéry, Antoine de, 17
Saki, 173
Salle, Antoine de, 16
Sand, George, 14, 18, 22, 28, 50, 62, 93, 171, 172
Schreiner, Olive, 29
Schumann, Robert, 54, 63, 65, 70
Schwarz, Oswald, 30
Shakespeare, William, 23, 40, 52, 54, 64, 85, 115, 186
Shaw, Bernard, 96, 128
Sheridan, Richard, 161
Smith, Alexander, 21
Smith, Revd Sydney, 92
Southerne, Thomas, 102
Southey, Robert, 71
Spark, Muriel, 35
Staël, Madame de, 26
Steele, Richard, 52, 116, 117, 135, 160, 175
Stendhal, 39, 46, 165, 168
Stewart, James, 182
Stopes, Marie, 153
Sullivan, Harry Stack, 29

Taylor, Bayard, 16
Taylor, Elizabeth, 134, 172
Tennyson, Alfred Lord, 172
Thackeray, W.M., 22, 23, 40, 65

Thoreau, Henry D., 25, 185
Thurber, James, 12
Tolstoy, Leo, 46, 57, 114, 124, 150
Tomick, Dave, 72
Townsend, Sue, 33
Traherne, Thomas, 14
Trollope, Anthony, 101, 106, 124, 150
Turgenev, Ivan, 34
Twain, Mark, 33
Tweedie, Jill, 20

Ustinov, Peter, 40

Van Dyke, Henry, 30
Victoria, Queen, 100, 111, 129, 137
Villiers, George, Duke of Buckingham, 29

Walker, James J., 55
Walpole, Hugh, 37, 57, 118, 154, 157, 182
West, Jessamyn, 19
West, Mae, 12, 87
Wharton, Edith, 65, 125, 130, 156, 184
White, E.B., 12
Wieck, Clara, 133
Wilde, Oscar, 58, 73, 102, 109, 110, 124
Williams, Tennessee, 15
Wilson, A.N., 21
Wodehouse, P.G., 120
Wolfe, Thomas, 63
Wollstonecraft, Mary, 112
Woolf, Virginia, 154
Wordsworth, William, 176
Wotton, Sir Henry, 182

Yeats, J.B., 27
Yeats, W.B., 183